UNDERGROUND CASE FILES PRESENTS

Thirty Pieces of Silver

By S. J. Short

ISBN-13: 978-1522756392
ISBN-10: 1522756396

This book goes out to all the fans of the works of Bram Stoker, Mary Shelly, Oscar Wilde, H. G. Wells and many other great writers who have made the classic monsters and characters we know today, and what things might be like if their stories were real and if their characters did exist.

CONTENTS

Chapter 1

The Gargoyles

The rain came down heavy and fast in London; Westminster Abbey stood alone and the rain had made the path up to the abbey doors glossy and wet.

A man walked up the path to Westminster Abbey, he must have been in his early twenties, he had brown hair and some might say he was handsome. He wore a grey pinstriped suit, he had a black walking stick and a black overcoat. He walked up the steps into Westminster Abbey and stepped inside. It was cold and dark inside the abbey. On the entrance wall at the top was a magnificent stained glass window; along the main hall were tall stone pillars which formed a hollow corridor filled with arches, and above the arches were chandeliers made of glass. Propped up on stone pedestals were amazingly carved stone Gargoyles. The Gargoyles were weird-looking creatures; they had the body of a lizard with chicken legs on the hind feet and lion feet on their two front feet, and the head of a human with wide opened eyes and their tongues sticking out.

Dorian Gray walked around the hall, his right hand clenched tightly around his walking stick; suddenly a loud, sharp crack came from Dorian's left. He turned around and saw, to his amazement, one of the Gargoyles missing. Dorian pulled out his sword from his walking stick and looked around the room; he had expected to find them here but was still amazed at how quickly they had become aware of him being here.

"Fancy us meeting him here," came a cold gravel-like voice.

"What does he want with us, I wonder?" came another voice. Dorian turned around and saw the Gargoyle that had stood on the pedestal on the right was gone; he looked up above him, he could hear something crawling along the ceiling.

"He doesn't know where to find us!" one of the Gargoyles laughed. Dorian pulled a small bottle out from his pocket, he knew he'd need this if he was going to go up against these creatures; he took the lid off and poured a clear-coloured liquid upon the blade of his sword.

"What is he doing now, we wonder?" said the other Gargoyle, as though this was all a game.

"Wouldn't you like to know," Dorian said aloud.

"Wouldn't we like to know," said the Gargoyle. "Wouldn't we like to know!" they repeated again and again, laughing out loud.

"I know you fled to England," Dorian told the Gargoyles, though he couldn't see them.

"He knows, he knows, he knows, he knows!" they both laughed.

"I've come to send you back to back to France," Dorian said, and the laughter stopped.

"No!" one of them shrieked. "He can't, they would kill us!"

"What you did over there was unacceptable and you must stand trial," Dorian told them.

"No!" cried one of the Gargoyles, and dived at Dorian out of nowhere; its face was screwed up in anger, eyes red.

Dorian waved his sword at the creature and slashed at it down the middle, leaving a long, deep scar. "Arrr!" the stone monster cried out in pain. A fine stream of steam came out of the wound as it burnt, deeper and deeper.

"He hurt us, he hurt our brother. The devil, the fiend, the monster!" said the other Gargoyle angrily.

"If you don't come quietly then I will harm both of you!" Dorian called out. No response came but then out of the darkness came a blood-piercing shriek from behind Dorian. He turned around and saw the other Gargoyle dive at him. Dorian was knocked off his feet, his sword fell from his hand as he was knocked to the ground – it had gone under a wooden church-style bench.

"You will not harm us!" the Gargoyle said to Dorian. It raised its arm and slashed at Dorian with its long, sharp claws which pierced Dorian's face. Four long scars appeared across his face for about ten seconds, then healed up in an instant.

"Not fair, that's cheating, cheating!" the wounded Gargoyle said across the room. The Gargoyle raised its arm up again ready for a second attack, but Dorian was quick; he grabbed the Gargoyle's raised arm by the wrist and flung him across the room and it smashed against one of the stone pillars. "Arrr!" it cried in pain.

Dorian got to his feet and ran for his sword. He picked his sword up off the ground and turned to face the Gargoyle that was now running for him. Dorian aimed his sword down at the creature as it dived for him, and Dorian stabbed it in the chest and it wailed in pain.

"How, how did it harm us?" asked the Gargoyle as it crawled towards Dorian with great pain and difficulty.

"Simple," Dorian told the Gargoyle, and pulled the small bottle out of his pocket.

"What is that?" the Gargoyle asked.

"Acid," Dorian said as he put it back in his coat pocket. "You're made of stone, nothing can harm you except for acid. Don't worry, you won't die," Dorian told the two Gargoyles as he put his sword back into his walking stick. "It will be sore for a couple of days but the pain should go away just in time for your return journey home." The Gargoyles started to cry. Dorian pulled a small black remote out of his other pocket and pressed the single black button and a red light flashed.

"Your escorts will be here in a few minutes," Dorian informed the Gargoyles, then left the abbey, leaving the creatures to cry alone in the dark.

Chapter 2

Jason Wilson

Jason Wilson woke that morning and got out of bed; he went into the bathroom and had a wash, after that he would get dried and put his school uniform on then go downstairs to have breakfast. Jason was a fifteen-year-old boy with light brown hair and dark green eyes. He ate his cereal and then picked up his bag and left for school.

"See you tonight, Mum," he told his mum, and kissed her on the cheek.

"Have a nice day," Jason's mum said to him as he walked out of the door. Jason walked alone to school.

He walked through Milsons Park; it was a luscious green park, full of trees and many beautiful flowers. He passed the children's playground and walked up the path to the gates at the end of the park. He opened the gate and left the park, then made his way to Milson Secondary School.

Jason arrived in time for his first lesson which was English; he sat at the back of the class, his books out and his pen in hand. Today they were given an assignment on writing a book review; they had all been given the choice of which book they could do.

Jason was doing a book review on *A Study in Scarlet* by Sir Arthur Conan Doyle.

"You and your mystery books," the girl sat next to him said. She had dark blonde hair and brown eyes.

"What's wrong with mystery books?" Jason asked her.

"Nothing," she replied, smiling. "I've just never known someone who reads mystery stories more than you," she told him.

"The trouble with you, Rachel, is that you read books about love and vampires but with lots of action, while I prefer my stories to have mystery, action, adventure, and excitement." Rachel smiled at him, she was probably the only friend he had in the class, well, the only friend who understood him better than anyone else in the school.

"I bet you're writing a review on Twilight," Jason said to her, trying to look at her paper.

"So what if I am?" she asked him, the smile still on her face.

"What do you even see in it?" Jason asked. "There's nothing romantic about vampires, they're cold-blooded killers," Jason told her.

"It's not just about people making out with vampires," Rachel explained to him.

"No, it's about vampires making out with people," Jason said, smiling.

"That's pretty much the same as what I said it wasn't about," Rachel told Jason. They remained silent for a moment while writing down what the book they were reviewing was about.

"Anyway, there's a Twilight movie on tonight. Why don't you come round to mine and watch it?" Rachel asked him.

"I can't," Jason told her. "I promised my mum I'd come straight home and help her take some boxes up into the attic," Jason explained to Rachel.

"Ok, fine, I guess you'll have to come round some other night instead," she told him.

"That would be nice," Jason replied, and the two carried on with their work.

Chapter 3

Trouble in Sheffield

Dorian had been called to Downing Street by the Prime Minister himself at half past five that morning. Dorian left his house at half six and arrived at Downing Street for quarter to seven. He waited outside the Prime Minister's office. Something was wrong, Dorian could feel it, and it wasn't like the Prime Minister himself to call Dorian unless something was really wrong.

He sat on a chair just next to the door to the Prime Minister's office, then a woman in a black jacket and skirt walked out of the office and went over to Dorian.

"The Prime Minister will see you now, Mr Gray," she told him, and Dorian entered the Prime Minister's office.

"Come on in, Mr Gray," the Prime Minister said.

Peter Cross was a man in his forties with curled black hair and a slim face; he was wearing a blue pinstriped suit and a red tie.

"Have a seat," he told Dorian, and Dorian sat on the chair that faced the Prime Minister's desk.

"It's not like you to call me here," Dorian said to Mr Cross as he straightened his suit jacket.

"I'm afraid this is urgent," Peter Cross said to Dorian in a serious tone. "Last night, we got reports that a Mr Amadeus Harfang arrived here in Britain," he told Dorian, handing him a file.

"Harfang the vampire? Impossible," Dorian said, alarmed. "He wouldn't come here, this is probably the only country in the world where he has no friends or allies, not that he ever did. He's an unlikeable person," he told the Prime Minister.

"Who is he anyway?" Cross asked Dorian. "I was only told that he was dangerous."

"He's a vampire fanatic," Dorian said. "One of the worst you'll ever find, even Dracula wishes to have nothing to do with him," Dorian explained.

"Well we have here a list of crimes he might have committed," Cross told Dorian, and Dorian took a list out of the file that he had just been given.

"Might have committed?" Dorian said, confused.

"Well no one has ever been able to arrest him because they had no evidence to prove it back in Europe," Cross explained, and turned to look out the window.

"Well that definitely sounds like Harfang – he doesn't leave a mess when he kills and definitely doesn't leave any clues, but I can't understand why he would come here," Dorian told Cross.

"I thought vampires didn't come here anymore," Cross said. He sounded frightened and had plenty of good reasons to be scared.

"They don't," Dorian replied. "They know this is the main land for Hunters such as myself," Dorian told Mr Cross. "But I'm confused," Dorian admitted. "Why have you called me to tell me he's here if he hasn't killed anyone yet?"

"He has," Cross replied, turning to face Dorian. "Last night a woman was found dead at a rubbish tip in Sheffield. The police haven't disturbed the crime scene but we need you there to tell the team that was sent there if this was Harfang's handiwork," Cross told Dorian.

"Alright," Dorian said, standing up, "I'll go down there at once," he told the Prime Minister.

"Hang on, Mr Gray," Cross said as Dorian was about to leave the room. "You'll be working with the lead detective on this case," he informed Dorian, then picked up his office phone to call his secretary. "Send her in," he said, and then a minute later, a woman with long black hair walked into the room; she had to have been in her late twenties or early thirties.

"This is Detective Kate Joan. Joan, this is Mr Dorian Gray." The two shook hands.

"I've read a lot about you, Mr Gray," she said to Dorian.

"It's a pleasure to meet you," Dorian replied, smiling.

"I suggest you two get straight down there," Cross said to both of them, and Dorian nodded.

"I'll keep you informed," Dorian told Cross, and they left the Prime Minister's office.

"So what do we know about the victim?" Dorian

asked Kate as they walked down the stairs, heading towards the way out.

"Nothing yet," Kate told him as they reached the front door.

"Have someone run our victim through missing persons' reports," Dorian told her as he opened the door for them to leave. "Knowing Harfang, he'll have kept her to feed on for at least a month."

"So how is it you know this guy?" Kate asked him as they walked down the street to Dorian's car.

"I've had a few dealings with him over the years," he said.

"So you must know him pretty well by now," Kate said.

"I do," Dorian replied.

They arrived at Dorian's car.

His car was a silver Mercedes with light brown leather seats. "Not bad," Kate said as they got in. A bag was on the back seat behind them.

"What's in the bag?" Kate asked him as he turned on the ignition.

"Work stuff," Dorian responded, and that was all he said on the subject.

They left Downing Street and drove down the road. Kate didn't know how but they had made it to Sheffield by half past eight and were making their way to the scene of the crime. "How did you do that?" Kate asked Dorian, amazed as they left a tunnel. "We were going through a tunnel in London and now we're in Sheffield."

Dorian smiled at her. "You'd be amazed at some of the tricks I've picked up over the years," he told her as they passed Wind Gardens.

"So where does this Amadeus Harfang come from?" Kate asked Dorian as they drove down Middlewood.

"Hard to say really," Dorian told her. "His origin is probably one of the few things I don't know about him but I know he speaks English, and as to which country he comes from, the last time I met him it was in Germany, 1945, just after the Second World War. I was sent to capture or kill him but I didn't get round to doing either, as he escaped and fled the country." They passed the Blue Ball pub and drove past trees. "How long have you been a detective in this line of work?" Dorian asked Kate.

"Three years," Kate said. "I was originally an officer at Scotland Yard, but one day a murder was reported and I was one of the first officers down there. It was horrible. I still think about it to this day, half the man's organs missing, his face was practically shredded to pieces, and then while I was digging deep into the investigation two men came around to my house and offered me a job. They took me with them to some kind of headquarters where a Mr Dwight explained to me about the existence of vampires and other kinds of fantasy creatures; he explained that the creature that had killed the man I was investigating was a werewolf and they offered me a job to work for them. Anyway, after I found the man or creature responsible I was promoted to detective and asked to work for Mr Dwight," she explained to him.

"I know Richard Dwight," Dorian said. "He's a

good man, excellent Caretaker, and I really mean that. He was the best man for the job when he got it eight years ago."

They soon arrived at the rubbish tip. It was closed, with police cars around it. Dorian and Kate got out of the car. Dorian was carrying his bag with him.

They both showed their badges to the officer at the gates and they were let in. Yellow police tape was hung up around the crime scene, a crime scene photographer was taking pictures, and a forensics officer was dusting for fingerprints on a yellow rubbish skip that was marked 'Green Garden Waste'. Inside the skip was a female body. She had brown hair with blood mixed in it, her eyes were closed and her skin pale white; two round puncture holes were in her neck, she wore a short green dress and black shoes. The pathologist who was working on this case walked over to Dorian and Kate. "Glad to see you both made it," he said to them both. He had bushy brown hair and wore glasses; he had grey eyes and was wearing a short white doctor's jacket.

"Mark," Kate said as he shook Dorian's hand, "this is Dorian Gray," she told him.

"Yes, I've heard a lot about you, Mr Gray," Mark said to Dorian.

"Thank you," Dorian replied. "What do we have here?" Dorian asked him as they walked over to the body.

"Well it's definitely a vampire killing, the bite mark is proof of that," he explained to them as he pointed to the bite marks on her neck.

"Did you check her eyes?" Dorian asked.

"Why?" Kate asked him, confused.

"I see what you mean," Mark said to Dorian.

"What are you both talking about?" Kate asked them both.

"Well, gypsies believe that a person captures the last few minutes of their life before they die, and that image is frozen in their eyes," Mark explained to Kate and Dorian opened his bag, pulled out a small bottle, and opened the victim's eyes. He poured a few drops of the clear liquid onto both eyes, then closed them.

"Hand me your phone," Dorian said to Kate. She handed him her phone and then Dorian opened the victim's eyes and a small image was in both eyes, but it was too small to make out what it was. Dorian took a picture of one of the eyes with Kate's phone, then handed it to Kate; she and Mark looked at the picture which had been enlarged when Dorian had taken it. A man in a black tailcoat and suit stood in the centre of the picture, but his face was covered by a hood; the only part of his face they could make out was his chin, which was pale white

"Harfang," Dorian said in a low voice.

"We can't be sure it was him," Kate said to Dorian.

"Of course we can!" Dorian told her sharply. "He arrived last night and this body was found in the early hours of this morning, far too close to be a coincidence if you ask me," he said to her.

"I don't mean he didn't do it but we'll have a hard time proving it was him since the man in this picture's face is hidden," Kate told Dorian.

"Well we definitely do know it's him. He doesn't like to leave any clues that could be traced back to him, one of the reasons we've never been able to get him," Dorian explained to her.

"Hang on," Mark said to them both as he looked more closely at the photo. "Look at the background, it looks like the cargo hold on a plane where people's suitcases are stored," he told them both.

"He's only just arrived in the country," Dorian said, realising what this might mean. "This woman wasn't killed here, she was taken from whichever country Harfang was in last so he had something to feed on while on the plane."

"Then why dump her body here?" Kate asked Dorian curiously.

"To throw us off his trail," Dorian told her. "He's not here in Sheffield, he knew this would be the first place we'd look if the body was found so he left it here and went someplace else."

"There's nothing else here," Mark told them. "If you two wouldn't mind, I'd like to take the body back to the morgue." Two assistants brought a stretcher out and with care, laid the body on the stretcher and carried it away to a medical examiner's van. They drove off as soon as Doctor Markus Barker got into the van.

Dorian and Kate were already driving back to London; Kate had just got off the phone and turned to Dorian. "That was one of the guys back at HQ, they've found out who our victim is," she said. "Her name is Marry Creed, she's twenty-one years old and is from Switzerland. According to the missing persons reports over there she disappeared about a month ago. Her parents have been informed and they're coming to collect their daughter's body."

Dorian looked at her then carried on driving. "What did they tell the parents about how their daughter died?" Dorian asked.

"They just said she was stabbed and bled to death," she told him. Suddenly Dorian's phone rang; he pulled over and pulled his smartphone out of his pocket.

"Hello," he said.

"Dorian, it's Dwight," the man said on the phone. "A werewolf was sighted in Milsons Park last night," he told Dorian.

"We'll get over there right away," Dorian replied and put his phone back in his pocket. "There's been a werewolf sighting back in London," Dorian informed Kate as they carried on driving.

"Where is it now?" Kate asked him.

"No idea, we'll have to wait for it to return tonight, with any luck it will return to Milsons Park," he explained to her.

"What about Harfang?" Kate said.

"He can wait," Dorian told her. "I don't need to tell you how much damage a single werewolf can do on its own," he said, and they rushed back to London.

Chapter 4

The Werewolf's Bite

School finished at five past three as usual; Jason had gone straight home to help his mum. He had got back home and changed out of his school uniform and into some jeans and a T-shirt, then went to help his mum out. She was standing on a ladder that led into the attic, a row of boxes waiting for her. "Could you pass me those up please?" she asked Jason.

Jason picked up the first box and handed it to her. "It's heavy," Jason said. "What's in it?"

"Your sister's trophies from school," she told him. Jason's sister, Juliet, was a bright teenager who had finished school last year and had gone to college. Jason only ever saw her once or twice a month. The college she had gone to was far on the other side of London and so she had bought a small apartment close to the college.

"Did she call today?" Jason asked as his mum shoved the box aside for some others in the attic.

"Yes, she called this afternoon; she said she's trying to get some free time so she can come home for a few days," she told him. He smiled as he passed her the next box.

"I was thinking of asking Rachel over one day next week," he told her.

"That's great!" his mum said, smiling. "It's been a while since you've had a friend over," she told him.

"What on earth is in these boxes?" Jason asked her. The boxes were extremely heavy.

"Just some of yours and Juliet's stuff from when you were little," she told Jason as she placed the box up in the attic.

It took them nearly an hour and a half to put all the boxes away in the attic and it was already starting to get dark outside. Jason and his mum ate their dinner alone – his dad was currently working away in America. He worked for a computer company and he had to go over to America to seal a deal with his new clients. Jason and his mum were having chicken stir fry and were sat at the dinner table. "Jason," his mum said as he drank his cocoa, "when you've finished, could you go down to the post box across the road and post this letter for me please?" She showed him a brown envelope. "It's that report your dad wanted me to send to the office while he's away," she explained to him.

"Ok," he said, and carried on eating.

Jason soon finished his dinner then put on his shoes and coat, then took the envelope and left. The post box was next to the entrance gate into Milsons Park. Jason walked up to the post box and slid the envelope in. Suddenly, a low growl could be heard coming from inside the park.

"Hello?" Jason said and stepped into the park. Standing there behind a tree was a wolf the size of a man with dark grey fur and pointed ears. Its sharp teeth were gleaming white, covered in blood, and its eyes were a dark, cold yellow with black pupils. The wolf was eating what looked like the remains of a squirrel, but then it stopped eating and lifted up its head and its nose wrinkled as it sniffed the night air. It knew Jason was there and Jason knew it knew he was there, and so he started to back away from the creature, not taking his eyes off it in case it turned around to look at him.

Dorian and Kate arrived at Milsons Park; two men in black police-style uniforms walked over to them. "It's in there, sir," one of the officers said. "We didn't dare confront it until you arrived."

"Good, wise move," Dorian said as he pulled his walking stick out of the car. "You might want to use these," Dorian told Kate and the two officers, and then handed Kate a small box full of silver bullets.

"Surely one bullet will suffice, sir?" the second officer said as he and the other officer started loading both their guns with silver bullets.

"It takes more than one bullet to take it down," Dorian explained to the second officer. "Silver bullets are the only bullets that can penetrate a werewolf's skin, but that's all, so I suggest you aim for the heart."

Once they finished loading their guns, Kate and the two officers followed Dorian into the park where it was dark and quiet. The trees stood tall and menacing and the leafless branches looked like bony fingers in the dark, reaching out for the stars and the moon. "Keep quiet now," Dorian whispered, "werewolves have sharp hearing,"

"I know that," Kate told Dorian in a low voice. "I've dealt with werewolves before, remember."

Suddenly they heard a low growl that was coming from straight ahead.

"I think it's up ahead, sir," the first officer said to Dorian.

"Ok, get ready people," Dorian instructed, and they advanced forward. Dorian pulled out his sword from his walking stick, ready for the fight.

The wolf turned around and saw Jason; it growled and revealed its teeth. Jason stepped back for the gate but tripped and fell onto the stone path. The wolf advanced and raised its left arm, its five fingers tipped with sharp claws, and swiped at Jason and cut him across his chest, leaving five long gashes. "Arrr!" Jason cried in pain. The wolf came in for another swipe but Jason placed his hand on a stick and swung it into the wolf's arm, and knocked it off the collision course with Jason's face. The wolf backed off a few steps; Jason got up and ran for the gate but just as he ran through the gate, the wolf dived at him, sinking its teeth into Jason's shoulder. "Arrr!" Jason cried in pain. He fell to the ground, blood dripping from his shoulder and chest. He felt like he was going to pass out and could hear the wolf behind him, coming in for another bite, but at that moment a gun shot went off and the wolf turned around and headed back into the park. Jason took his chance and got up and ran as fast as he could for home.

Kate had seen the werewolf and it looked as if it was heading out of the park. They couldn't let that happen; they couldn't afford for it to get out and hurt an innocent person, so she had fired her gun into the air to try and get the wolf's attention. It had worked, the wolf had turned around and was heading for them now – fast – and it growled loudly, and the growling got louder as it got closer to them. Then it attacked them.

"Duck!" Dorian shouted as it dived at them. Kate and the two officers dived to the ground and the wolf flew over them and landed on its feet. It turned and looked at them, it snarled and ran at them, but Dorian came at the wolf. Dorian rammed his walking stick into the wolf's side and it fell down on its opposite side. Dorian pointed his sword at the wolf's chest and was ready to stab it when it swung its arm at him and Dorian was knocked off his feet. He hit a tree and slumped down onto the ground.

The wolf got up and went over to Dorian; it growled and raised its arm, ready to strike again, but then there was a gun shot and the wolf fell to the ground, howling in pain. Dorian looked up and saw Kate standing there with her gun aiming at where the wolf had stood.

"Nice shot," Dorian said to her as he got up and saw where she had shot the wolf, a bullet hole was at the bottom of his back, in the spine, which must have crippled the wolf.

"What are we going to do with it?" the second officer asked as he and the first officer got up off the grass.

"Take him back to base where he'll receive medical aid and await trial, and then possibly either execution or imprisonment," Dorian explained.

Kate had called for a van to take the wolf back to HQ and have it examined by a medical team and then locked up. "We only got here just in time," Dorian told Kate as he sat down next to her on a bench in the park.

"You're right," Kate said as they watched the van take the werewolf away, "it might have infected anyone."

"Are you alright?" Dorian asked Kate. "You seem disturbed."

"I didn't know him, Dorian," she said. "He could have been a good person, with a job, wife, and kids and I just shot him." She looked at Dorian, upset.

"You had no choice, he was out of control," Dorian told her, getting up off the bench. "C'mon," he said to her. "Tomorrow we pick up where we left off with the Harfang case."

Kate looked at him and got up.

"How long have you been around?" Kate asked Dorian as they began to walk back to his car."

"That's rather personal, but if you must know, since 1845, but if you mean how long have I been immortal, then since 1866," he said. They reached the car.

"But your book didn't come out until 1890," Kate said, confused, as they got in the car.

"Oscar had it published that year so no one would ever suspect I was real," Dorian explained as they left Milsons Park. "Look on the bright side," Dorian said as they drove down the road, "at least no one got hurt."

Jason staggered towards his home; he had lost a lot of blood and he felt like he was going to pass out. There must have been something in that wolf's bite because it was burning like it was infected. He reached the front door, opened it and stepped inside. "You've been a long..." his mother was saying when he came in but at that moment, Jason had passed out on the floor. "Oh my god, Jason!" his mum said and rushed over to him and knelt down beside him, then pulled out her phone and called for an ambulance.

Chapter 5

Infection

Jason was rushed straight to hospital where the doctors were able to stop the bleeding but that didn't help Jason, his temperature had risen and he wasn't waking up, so the doctors began running tests on him.

Mrs Wilson was sat outside the room Jason was being kept in, her tissue was drenched in tears and she was still crying. "Mrs Wilson," a doctor said as she approached Mrs Wilson. "I'm Dr Kelly Brown," she told Mrs Wilson and sat next to her. "We've managed to stop the bleeding but he has a fever and his temperature has raised extremely high," she explained to Jason's mum.

"Has he woken up yet?" she asked Dr Brown.

"Not yet but he has lost a lot of blood, Mrs Wilson, he's lucky to even be alive," Dr Brown explained. "We're running every test there is to try and find out what's wrong with him."

Mrs Wilson wiped her eyes then looked at Dr Brown again. "Do you at least know what attacked him?" she asked Dr Brown.

"It's hard to say," Dr Brown explained. "The claw marks suggest a lion or a panther but the bite marks would suggest a large dog or wolf. The claws and the bite marks suggest two different types of animal."

A male nurse came out of Jason's room and turned to Mrs Wilson and Dr Brown. "He's woken up now," he told them both, and Mrs Wilson rushed past the nurse and went into Jason's room.

Jason looked terrible, he was pale and sweating although he felt cold; his mother wrapped her arms around him and hugged him. "Oh Jason, I thought I had lost you!" she was saying.

"Mum, I'm alright, you can let go now," Jason told her and she let go of him.

"Jason, I'm Dr Brown. I'd like to keep you in for a few days so we can run some tests on you," Dr Brown said to Jason as she picked up his medical file to read.

"Do you remember anything that happened to you?" she asked Jason.

"I went to post a letter for my mum, when I heard something in the park, next thing I know I'm being attacked by some kind of wolf. I tried to fend it off but when I turned to run it bit me and I don't remember what happened then."

"It's late; I suggest you get some rest," Dr Brown told him and then turned to his mum. "It might be best if you go home and get some rest too, Mrs Wilson. We'll let you know if anything happens." Jason's mum hugged and kissed him, then followed Dr Brown out of the room.

Jason lay down; he was still trying to get a grip on what had happened that night in the park and why he still couldn't stop thinking about it. He was also getting a strange feeling inside him, as if something about him was changing, something that could mean the beginning of something new.

Chapter 6

Amadeus Harfang

HQ has had four names over the years, originally called the Underground in 1850 but the name was changed in 1870 when the London underground was first built, and then HQ's name was changed to the Hive in 1872; but the name never caught on so it was changed again to the Underground Hunters in 1878, and then it was changed to HQ and had stayed that way ever since.

Dorian and Kate entered the HQ; it was built under Parliament and was made partly of the World War Two war rooms. The entrance into HQ used to be stairs but was changed to an elevator in 1947. The entrance room's walls were a tan brown colour and the floor had stone black tiles with a dark red rug in the centre. In the middle of the room was a dark brown wooden reception desk. A man sat at the reception desk; young, probably nineteen years old with dark ginger hair; he wore a black suit jacket over a green t-shirt and he also wore jeans and white sports trainers. "We're here to see Mr Dwight," Kate said to the secretary.

The secretary looked through his appointment

book. "He's expecting you," the secretary told Kate and Dorian. They went through the door on their left and walked down a long corridor. Two men were standing beside the water cooler looking over some crime scene photos. "It looks like a zombie to me pal," one of them said as Dorian and Kate walked past.

"It can't be, there's been no reports of zombies since 1967 in America," the other one replied. Dorian and Kate turned and came to Dwight's office, Dorian knocked on the door and they were called in.

Richard Dwight had ginger hair and he was roughly the same height as Kate. He wore a white shirt with his black tie loose and he also wore a black waistcoat, dark grey trousers, and black shoes. He sat at his desk with his glasses on, his laptop on and a stack of files in front of him. "Take a seat," he told Dorian and Kate; they sat down and looked at him. "I think we've found him," Dwight told them both and handed them the top file.

"How did you find him?" Dorian asked, amazed.

Dwight smiled. "Harfang paid for the flight to London, he wasn't a stowaway like we thought," Dwight explained and showed them a flight list.

"Do we know where he's been this past fifty years?" Dorian asked him as he read the flight list.

"Bulgaria, or at least that's where he took his flight to London from."

"Where is he now?" Kate asked.

Dwight looked at her. "One of our undercover agents spotted him arriving at St. Andros church last night," Dwight explained.

"That doesn't make sense," Kate said, confused. "Why would he hide at an old church? He knows he can't kill on holy ground."

"Because we can't kill him either," Dorian told her. "Vampires can't kill in the house of God because they are forbidden to by holy rights, and we must also abide by these rules too. A church is the only place where a vampire and a human can meet without trying to kill one another."

Kate looked at Dorian, astonished. "How do you know that?" she asked him, amazed.

"I was taught by Professor Van Helsing himself," Dorian told her. Now Kate was impressed by her immortal partner. "He was a good man and a good friend," he said at last. Dorian never talked about his past. Dwight, who had known Dorian since he was a young Hunter in training, had never even recalled Dorian telling him about his past. "Well we'd best be off," Dorian told Dwight as he and Kate got up.

"Where do you think you're going?" Dwight said, looking at them both, one eyebrow raised.

"I'm going to make a call in at Harfang's," Dorian told Dwight.

"Have you gone mad?" Dwight said, shocked. "We don't have a reason to call on him," Dwight said, standing up from his desk.

"We know it was him who murdered the girl we found at the tip and we know he's up to something," Kate told Dwight.

"Which we have no proof of," Dwight replied.

"We have the picture I took from the dead girl's

eyes," Dorian said, annoyed with Dwight holding him back.

"We have a picture of a hooded vampire, not necessarily Harfang!" Dwight responded quickly.

"Richard, we've been trying to get this monster for the past hundred and fifty years, well I have, but why am I still finding it hard to believe that you of all people are willing to just let Harfang walk away with murder!"

Dwight took off his glasses and rubbed his head. "Dorian I want him behind bars just as much as you do but he's killed far too many Hunters in the past who tried to arrest him. I know he won't be able to kill you but what about Detective Joans? What's to stop Harfang from ripping her up?"

Dorian let go of the door handle and turned back to look at Dwight. "Richard, you've known me long enough to know that I would never want to get any of my friends or partners hurt," Dorian said.

Dwight looked at him then put his glasses back on, "I know you wouldn't, you never have done," and with that, Dorian and Kate left Dwight's office and made their way to St. Andros church.

St. Andros was first built in 1664 but after the great fire of London in 1666 the church and nearly all of London had to be rebuilt. In 1950 the church was closed and never opened again but as long as it stood there it was still a house of God, and the perfect place for a vampire to stay if they didn't want a Hunter or anyone else coming to cut off their head. Dorian and Kate walked to the church. It stood alone in the middle between a Starbucks and a Waterstones book store; the church had two floors and was a dull stone grey colour. The cross that stood above the front doors had been removed. "Well we definitely know Harfang's here," Kate said, pointing at where the cross used to be. They went round to the back of the church where there was a back door and two windows, one on the bottom floor and one on the top floor. The top floor window was open with the curtains sticking out.

"Right, I'm going in," Dorian told Kate and handed her his walking stick and overcoat and started claiming up the drain pipe.

"You can't be serious!" Kate said, shocked. "What if Harfang's up there?" she asked him as he grabbed hold of the window ledge.

"Then tell Dwight I died of my own stupidity," Dorian said and climbed into the building.

"You can't die," Kate replied, annoyed.

"Then stop worrying!" Dorian said, and walked away from the window.

The room he was now in was small, full of wooden crates. Dorian opened one of the crates – it was full of old artefacts, no doubt Harfang's own private collection of dark artefacts dating to early vampire years before even Dracula's time. In the corner was a small freezer unit. Dorian opened it and inside were gallons and gallons of blood in glass containers. "He's here," Dorian said to himself, then shut the freezer. He walked over to the door leading out of the room and stepped out into an upstairs hallway. It was dark and the only light came from two candles. The wallpaper on the walls was old and had lost its colour years ago, and was starting to peel off the wall. Dorian walked down the hall, the wooden floor creaking silently with every step he took. Dorian came to the stairs and walked down them; he came to an open door at the bottom of the stairs and walked out into main hall of the church where people came to pray, but no one had come here in years.

The crosses, the religious statues, even the bibles that had been left behind when the church closed had been removed from this building. Even the mural painting of Christ on the cross had been scraped off the wall above the stained glass windows, which were now boarded up with wood to stop the sun coming through. It upset Dorian to see the church in this state; he had been christened here when he was just a baby and had come here with his mother and father right up to the day he had sold his soul and become immortal, but he still respected the religion, even if he no longer had a soul. Suddenly a door opened at the back of the room. Dorian went back the way he came, closed the door, and knelt down beside it, listening to what was happening.

Amadeus Harfang was tall, thin, and had white hair and pale white skin. He wore a black tailcoat and black suit trousers, he had a crisp white shirt with a black tie and black shoes, and he also wore a cape. He looked like your basic vampire except for the collar on the cape, and he didn't have black hair or a Transylvanian accent. Behind him were two zombies – they were men and looked like perfectly normal people except for the fact they had pale skin. One wore a trench coat stained with mud and dry blood – he had black hair. The other one wore a long blue doorman coat with black buttons and black boots and he was bald with a scar across his face. "Are you sure you want to go out tonight, sir?" the bald zombie asked. He was German and looked as though he belonged to some form of military group. "I can always send one of the others out and find someone for you."

"No," Harfang said, his cape sweeping the floor as he turned around to face them both. "I have had lesser creatures bring me my food ever since we left Bulgaria. I must go out and feast. I long to go out into the crowded streets where I can't be noticed, where I can slip away into the shadows and feast. I am not a monster that you cage up, Crown."

Crown, the bald zombie, bowed. "Of course, sir. I simply mean, is it safe for you to step out of the shadows yet?" Crown said and looked up at his master.

"You have always been a good friend, Crown," Harfang replied, "but I must go out. How can I complete what I came here to do on an empty stomach?" he asked Crown, then turned to walk down towards what would have been the vicar's office.

"Shall I have your morning meal brought to you, sir?" Crown asked as he watched his master leave.

"No," Harfang replied. "I will fetch it myself; the last zombie you sent to get my food has not yet come back." Harfang turned and went to the stairs; Crown turned to the zombie in the trench coat.

"Where has the zombie I sent to prepare Harfang's meals gone anyway?" Crown asked the zombie.

"Decaying in the back room," he replied.

"What do you mean?" Crown asked, confused. The zombie in the trench coat tossed Crown a small medicine bottle – it had a blue liquid inside.

"The idiot forgot to take his medication," the zombie explained.

"Fools!" Crown said, annoyed. "Did you even bother to tell them they would die permanently if they do not take the formula?"

"Of course I did!" the zombie replied, then walked off to the back room. "God! Someone needs to clean that guy up!" he said as he entered the back room.

Dorian had rushed back upstairs to the storage room. He went inside, closed the door, and headed to the window, but he knocked over a glass container full of blood as he hurried for the window. It smashed on the floor, blood trailed everywhere, footsteps could be heard, hurrying to find out what had smashed; the door handle turned.

Harfang was walking up the stairs. He disliked churches, humans praying to an almighty God just made him feel sick. Humans would pray to a God they had never met but if they knew of the existence of vampires they would cower like mice. But being in this building had its advantages; no one would try and kill him here, even though he couldn't kill them. Suddenly he heard a smash in the storage room. He quickened his pace and came to the top of the stairs. He walked down the corridor and turned the door handle, then entered the room; no one was there. A bottle of blood had been smashed on the floor; he would get one of the zombies to pick it up. He went over to the freezer and opened it up and took out a vial of blood. He drank it down in one gulp then threw the empty vial to the floor – it smashed. He started to walk out of the room when something caught his eye. He turned around and saw something hanging on one of the crates, it was a handkerchief with initials stitched in. The initials were DG. Harfang's eyes filled with anger and he felt like he could kill someone. Dorian Gray had found him.

Chapter 7

Someone's in Trouble

Harfang stormed back into the main hall of the church, all the zombies were waiting for him.

"We heard you scream, master," Crown said as Harfang approached.

"I have good reason to!" Harfang replied and stuffed the handkerchief into Crown's hand. "We've been discovered!" Harfang told Crown and the others. "Dorian Gray has found us. It will only be a matter of time until every single Hunter in Britain is after me!" Harfang was angry; half the zombies backed away.

"How did he find us?" Crown said, confused. "We covered our tracks well; they wouldn't expect you to come into the country using your real name."

"Unless," Harfang said, "unless they found the girl, then they would suspect me and someone must have spotted us arriving the other night." He turned to Crown. "Where did you put the body?" Harfang asked Crown.

"I was already busy dealing with the transportation of your coffin to be brought here," Crown explained, "so you gave the task to…"

"Blake!" Harfang shouted as he walked over to Blake; Blake was a short man with short hair and a lip piercing. "Where did you put the body?" Harfang asked Blake. He clutched both of Blake's arms.

"I dumped it at a tip in Sheffield, sir," Blake said nervously. "You just dumped it there? You fool! What did I tell you? I told you not to leave it where it might draw suspicion and you leave it at a rubbish tip!" Harfang clutched Blake's throat tightly in his hand.

"Please sir, it, it won't happen again," Blake squealed.

"You're right, it won't," Harfang said gently, and then tore Blake's throat out, and then dug his hand into his bare throat and pulled the spine out. Blake dropped to the floor, dead.

Harfang turned to Crown, Blake's spine still in his hand. "Get someone to clean that up!" he told Crown. "And then send some of the men out to keep a close eye on Mr Gray and the rest of the Hunters."

"Yes sir," Crown replied, and took the spine out of Harfang's hand and threw it onto Blake's body. "Clean that up!" he ordered the other zombies, and then followed Harfang out of the room.

Chapter 8

A Night Out

Jason was sent home after two days of tests and x-ray scans. Jason had spent all day in his room with his books, his DVDs, and his homework that Rachel had brought him that afternoon after school.

He was finishing his homework when his mum came up with his dinner. She had brought him soup. "Thanks Mum," Jason said as he took the tray off her.

"Your sister called to see if you were alright," his mum told him as he ate his dinner, "and your dad's tried to get back from America earlier than originally planned so he can come and see you," she explained. "I'll be downstairs if you need anything, just shout me," she told him then left his room.

At half nine, Jason fell asleep. His mum had come into his room and taken the bowl and tray away. It was quarter to twelve now, his mum had gone to bed an hour and a half ago. Jason woke up. He couldn't sleep, the bite marks were burning and that feeling he started to feel at the hospital had come back, and it was stronger this time. It was dark in his room; the only light in there was from the moon that shone through the window. Moonlight! Jason got out of bed and walked over to the window. He opened the window and the night air blew on his face, and then it hit him. The pain, the pain came. It started at his bite marks, then spread all over his body from his skin, to his teeth, in his bones, and in his muscles. Jason screwed his face up in pain; he wanted to scream but he couldn't quite get his voice to work.

Suddenly he felt his bones crack, as they grew and he changed size. His fingers were lengthening and his nails were turning into claws; fur was growing out of his skin around his neck, all over his face, on his back, around his waist, under his clothes and all over his legs. His feet were lengthening as well, and his toenails turned into claws just like his fingernails, and his face was changing.

Jason once again tried to scream in pain; his face formed a muzzle and his teeth grew into fangs and canine-like teeth. His ears became pointed like a dog or a wolf, his shoulders broadened, and muscle began to grow all over his body.

The pain soon ended. Jason had fallen to his knees, he felt... he didn't know how he felt but it was a completely new feeling. He got to his feet; he was taller and he felt uneasy on his feet – he nearly tripped over twice and had to grab hold of his wardrobe, but tripped over backwards as he saw his refection in the mirror that was attached to the wardrobe door.

The reason Jason's body had been in so much pain was because he had changed his physical form – he had become a werewolf. Jason stared at his reflection. What he saw horrified him. He had grown to seven foot tall with dark grey fur and tough skin, like rhino or elephant skin, and he had sharp black claws on his hands and feet (paws). His face looked like a wolf's face but more ferocious, with sharp yellow teeth and dark yellow eyes with cold black pupils. He had a black nose which picked up every scent in the house at this very moment, but the thing that freaked him out the most was that his body was made of pure solid muscle. He could see himself in the mirror and how unsettling it was to see this creature that was half man, half beast, with its body of knotted muscle and leathery skin and animal-like features which frightened Jason so much. He wished he could just wake up from this nightmare but alas, it was no nightmare, this had really happened. Jason clasped his hands around his face; tears ran down and wet the fur on his face but the sadness was short-lived and he was no longer Jason Wilson. No longer human, but a creature of the night.

The wolf stood in the bedroom; it looked around this prison of a room he was in and saw the open window. The wolf approached the window and peered out into the night sky and sniffed the air. He could smell the scent of small squirrels nearby in the trees and the smell of humans all around him. It was like an open feast. The wolf climbed out of the window and crouched on the window sill and gazed up at the moon; finally howling up at the moon like something out of a black and white horror film.

Suddenly there was movement in the garden below, squirrels no doubt searching for food. The wolf dived off the window sill and landed with its feet on the ground. He lowered his head as he sniffed for the squirrel; he picked up its scent. The squirrel was running across the ground, a berry in its mouth, when suddenly the wolf pounced on it and scooped it up in its mouth, and before the squirrel had time to fight back, the wolf bit down on the squirrel, snapping its spine and killing it in one go. The wolf chewed then swallowed the dead squirrel, it licked around its mouth, cleaning up any blood that might have squirted out.

Suddenly there was another noise behind the wolf. It turned around and saw another squirrel, but this one was quick, it darted across the ground and climbed up a tree as quickly as it could climb. The wolf watched it disappear into the trees, then the wolf went and climbed over the garden fence. It had picked up a new scent, the scent of humans, and lots of them.

Fletcher Thompson was walking through the park. He was a thirty-five year old man, who lived in a flat and worked as a salesman. He was walking home from the pub when he heard a rustle in the bushes. He turned in the direction of the noise, nothing there, so he carried on walking, unaware that a werewolf was following him. Thompson stopped again when he heard a low growl behind him, he spun around and saw the wolf standing in front of him, standing on two legs, seven foot tall, and it was snarling at him. Thompson turned and ran, trying to put as much distance between him and that thing as he possibly could, but the wolf was fast. It dived on him and bit his throat, crushing his windpipe; he was dead in a matter of seconds.

The wolf began to feast on the man he had just killed. It ate and it ate, every single organ he could find in the man's chest. The wolf ate the liver and both the kidneys and was moving on to the stomach when he heard the sound of people coming. For one brief moment he thought, *More food*, but realised that more people meant a better fighting chance, so the wolf just ripped out the first organ he could get his teeth around and then left as fast as it could, before people saw it.

The wolf returned to the house it had come from and climbed up the wall and in through the open window, into the empty room it had come from; it crawled onto the empty bed and curled up in a ball, then fell asleep.

Chapter 9

Another Werewolf!

It was four o'clock in the morning, Kate was asleep. When her phone rang she woke up, turned on the lamp, then rubbed her eyes. She picked up her phone, it was Dorian. She answered it. "Kate here," she said.

"You're not going to like this," Dorian said to her. Judging by the sounds in the background, he was back at HQ. "We just got reports of another werewolf sighting in Milsons Park earlier this morning," he informed her. Kate groaned then got out of bed.

"But we took out the wolf, he's back at HQ. Mark said that the doctors back at the Underground had it sedated," Kate said as she pulled out her jeans and jacket.

"Obviously there's more than one," Dorian replied. He sounded as though he was leaving the Underground. "I'm heading down to Milsons Park now, I take it I'll meet you there?" he asked her.

"I'm on my way," she said, and put down the phone, and then started to get dressed.

Kate arrived at Milsons Park at twenty to five. The whole area had been sealed off to the public with yellow crime scene tape and police officers were standing watch at the entrance to the park. Kate showed them her badge and they let her pass. Mark and Dorian were waiting for her in the park; they were standing over the remains of a body. "Definitely a werewolf attack," Mark told Kate as she approached.

"It looks more like a werewolf feast," Kate said as she stood beside Dorian.

"Clearly there's more than one werewolf around here," Dorian said to Kate.

"I take it the Harfang case will have to go on hold until we've found the other werewolf?" Mark asked them both as the coroners came and took the remains of the body away.

"No," Dorian told him. "Harfang's more of a threat than a werewolf."

"I think Dwight might disagree with you there," Kate said to Dorian.

Dorian looked at her, then looked at Mark. "We need to talk to the werewolf we caught the other night," Dorian told him.

"I think he's awake now, you can go back and see him if you like," Mark said as he followed the coroners to the coroner van.

Dorian and Kate arrived back at HQ and entered the medical room; a doctor was sat at a desk writing a medical report. "We'd like to talk with the wolf," Dorian told the doctor.

"His name is Mr Alan Crest, he's thirty-five years old

and has a wife and a child," the doctor informed him.

"Very well," Dorian said. "We'd like to talk with Mr Crest."

"Of course," the doctor replied and led them to a room. Inside was Alan Crest. He was a man in his mid-thirties with black hair and grey eyes; his wife was sat on a chair next to the bed he was lying in. His wife was the same age but with blonde hair and green eyes – she seemed worried.

"Mr Crest, I'm Dorian Gray," Dorian told Crest as he sat opposite him and his wife.

"Like the immortal guy out of that film?" Crest asked Dorian.

"I am that guy," Dorian replied, "and yes, I am immortal, but my friend here isn't. Detective Kate Joan, the leading detective on our current case that you have become involved in," Dorian explained.

"I'm the one who shot you," Kate told Crest. Crest's wife looked shocked.

"Did I hurt anyone?" Crest asked them both worriedly.

"No," Kate replied, "but recently there's been another werewolf attack, this one killed a man. We were wondering if…"

"I had anything to do with it?" Crest said. "I'm used to people accusing me of attacking people, Detective, but I haven't changed for nearly three years now," Crest explained to them. "When Chelsea and I found out we were having a baby, I started taking medication for my condition. I had been taking it before but we couldn't always afford it, so I left my old job and took up a job at Cal's Computer Programming. I started to make more money, which was good because Chelsea had to go onto maternity leave."

"If you were on medication then why did you change?" Dorian asked Crest.

"I don't know why, my medication hasn't been working as well lately," Crest explained. "Two nights ago, I felt the change coming and so Chelsea and my son left for her mother's that night and I spent the night alone."

"Do you have your medication on you?" Kate asked Crest.

"Yes," Crest's wife said, and handed Kate a small green bottle half full of tablets. Kate examined the bottle then handed it to Dorian, who took one out and placed it on the floor, then crushed it with tip of his walking stick. He dipped his index finger in the powder of what remained of the tablet and tasted it.

"It's salt," he told them. "You were given fake tablets," Dorian said to Crest. "Who gave you these?"

"I got them from the pharmacist here at HQ," Crest told Dorian. "Normal pharmacists don't supply them."

"Who gave them to you?" Dorian repeated.

"A man at the pharmacist, he was different to the usual guy, he was pale-skinned and bald," Crest said.

"Did he talk in a German accent?" Dorian asked.

"Yes," Crest replied.

"Damn it!" Dorian shouted and threw the bottle of

tablets across the room. "That man you described is Amadeus Harfang's number one man. His name is Crown and he is a German war criminal." Dorian slammed his walking stick on the wall. "Harfang planned all this to keep us distracted," he told Kate. Suddenly Mark came into the room, a folder in his hand.

"Excuse me Mr Crest, do you remember a thing about the night we brought you in?" Mark asked Crest.

"No," Crest replied. "I don't."

"Because we found blood on your teeth before you changed back to human form," Mark told Crest.

"Whose blood?" Dorian asked.

"We couldn't get an identity, there was too much saliva mixed in with the blood, but we were able to find out it was male blood," he told Kate and Dorian.

"Thank you for your time," Kate said to Mr and Mrs Crest, then left the room with Mark.

They walked out of the medical bay and down a corridor. "So what now?" Kate asked Dorian.

"You're the lead detective on this case," Dorian told her as they turned a corner. Mark was trying to keep up with them.

"I mean do we go after Harfang or the werewolf?" she asked.

"The werewolf of course," Dorian said, then stopped outside a filing room.

"So what do we do now, detective?" Dorian asked Kate, leaning on his walking stick.

"Obviously the werewolf is a local in the area we found the body," Kate told Dorian.

"We caught Alan Crest in Milsons Park but he lives downtown. What are the chances this werewolf lives anywhere near Milson?" Dorian asked. Kate shrugged. "Ok, we set up a surveillance team and wait for the werewolf to strike again."

"Actually guys, there's no full moon tonight," Mark informed them, Dorian and Kate looked at him.

"That only happens in movies," Dorian told him. "A real werewolf doesn't need the full moon, it can transform as long as it isn't a half moon and that's not for another two days," Kate explained to Mark.

"So we set up a surveillance squad," Mark said, and Dorian and Kate nodded. "Ok," Mark said, "I'm going to go back to my lab and see if we can find out anything else about our other werewolf," then Mark went back to his lab.

Chapter 10

Guilty

Jason woke up late in the morning. He slowly got out of bed then slumped to the floor; his face was covered in sweat. Last night he had had the weirdest dream and it wasn't something he would be forgetting anytime soon.

He got out of bed and went over to the mirror; his shirt was on the floor, ripped. Jason picked it up and placed it in his bedroom bin, then turned to face the mirror and to his horror, he discovered his dreams had been real. He was covered in blood and his pyjama bottoms were tattered and torn. Jason went pale in the face, he backed away from the mirror slowly, and slumped down onto the floor. What had he done and who had he attacked? He was scared, more scared than he had ever been in his life.

He didn't know what to do; he needed a shower, that much he knew. His mother was downstairs so he didn't pass her on the landing. He threw his shorts in the bin and went into the bathroom to have a wash. All he had to hope now was that he wasn't in any trouble, but he needed help and he needed it fast.

Chapter 11

Watch Duty

Kate had set up two surveillance teams, one covering the park entrance and the other covering the park exit. Mark, who had been working hard on trying to identify the werewolf, had been able to set up some monitors in the park in case the werewolf got in without them knowing.

"Nothing yet," Mark told her as he read the monitors' readings on his iPad.

"What do you expect? It's still day," Kate told him.

Mark looked out the window then turned back to Kate, realising they were missing someone. "Where's Dorian?" he asked Kate.

"I don't know, he said he had something he had to do," she explained.

"He seems very determined about this case," Mark said as a group of college students passed, all five of them laughing.

"He's been after Harfang for years, ever since 1912 I think," Kate told Mark.

"It's hard to believe he's lived this long, he looks

younger than most of the new officers at the HQ," Mark replied.

"I think he's been married once or twice too," Kate said.

"Unbelievable," Mark said.

They sat there for another half hour and then Kate finally spoke again. "It's getting near to lunch, do you want to get us something from Subway?" Kate asked Mark.

"Sure, what do you want?" he asked as he undid his seatbelt.

"Anything as long as it's not tuna, I can't have fish," Kate replied.

"Ok," Mark said, then got out the car then walked off towards the Subway across the road.

Crown and another zombie watched as the pathologist left the car that he had been sat in with the detective. "No sign of the immortal guy," the zombie told Crown.

"He's got to be there somewhere," Crown said, annoyed. Dorian was the man who had killed him during World War Two. Harfang had helped Crown once or twice in the war and it was Harfang who had brought him back as a zombie, but by the time Crown had come back, Germany had lost the war. Crown may not have agreed with the reasons why his country had gone to war but this wasn't about that, Dorian had killed him and after he came back as a zombie his own wife and children were terrified of him. Now Crown had sworn vengeance for what Dorian had done to him.

Chapter 12

The Hunter Becomes

the Hunted

Dorian was checking through records of registered werewolves in London – nearly all of them were dead. Except for three, one of them being Alan Crest, of course. The other two had moved to different countries; one had moved to Miami in America and the other had moved to Australia.

Dorian sat back in his chair and rubbed his forehead. "Stuck, are we?" Dwight said. He had been standing by the door way of the records room watching Dorian.

"You have no idea," Dorian replied.

"Maybe you need a fresh pair of eyes on this," Dwight told Dorian.

"I'm alright," Dorian said as he opened another set of files.

"Dorian, you've been at this nearly all day and despite all appearances, I'm still younger than you." Suddenly Dorian froze.

"Dorian?" Dwight asked.

"Younger!" Dorian shouted as he jumped to his feet. "Dwight, you're a genius!" Dorian said as he left the room.

"What did I say?" Dwight asked him.

"The reason this werewolf won't be in the records is because he's young and possibly only just been bitten!" Dorian ran down the corridor, pulled out his phone from his pocket and called Kate to tell her what he had just discovered.

That night, Kate and Mark met up with Dorian at Milsons Park, where it was cold and starting to get foggy. "Great," Mark said miserably, "we're about to go and hunt a werewolf and it's foggy, how could this get any worse?"

"Stop moaning," Kate replied as she zipped up her jacket.

"Right," Dorian said, clearing his throat, "we all know what to do if we see the werewolf?" Dorian asked them both.

"We hit it with these darts," Mark replied, showing a tranquiliser gun to Dorian.

"Excellent, remember it might be a kid we're dealing with so no killing."

"Let's go," Kate said, and they all split up. Kate took the main path leading to the front gates of the park. It was dark and quiet, nothing was stirring, not even the leaves were moving in the wind on this particularly windy night. Suddenly something moved in the shadows. Kate aimed her tranquiliser gun at the darkness but nothing moved. Kate slowly lowered her gun then walked off.

Dorian was on the biker's path across from the duck pond. Dorian stopped suddenly in his tracks; he thought he could hear something. He turned to face a bush and Dorian drew his sword from his walking stick and poked about in the bushes. Suddenly something leapt out. Dorian pulled out his tranquiliser gun and to his relief, saw a squirrel. "Bloody thing!" Dorian said, then carried on walking down the path.

Mark was patrolling the path leading out of the park when he heard something in the trees; he looked up and for a brief second saw the wolf climbing up the tree. Mark quickly pulled out his walkie-talkie. "It's up in the old oak tree near the park exit!" Mark said quietly.

"We're on our way," Dorian replied.

Suddenly the werewolf leapt out of the tree and into the dark. Mark pulled out his tranquiliser gun and hid behind the tree. He could hear the beast's breath and he could hear it growl. Mark readied his gun and was prepared to fire it when he heard it come towards him. Quickly he turned and fired, but he hadn't hit the wolf, it was Kate he had hit. She collapsed to the ground, unconscious. Mark cursed under his breath. He reloaded his gun and searched for the wolf but it had gone.

"What happened to Kate?" Dorian asked when he arrived.

"I kind of shot her," Mark admitted.

Dorian looked at him. "You shot her!" Dorian said, a look of disbelief on his face.

"I thought she was the wolf," Mark added quickly.

"You shot her!" Dorian repeated. "You idiot, you absolute incompetent idiot!" Dorian said to Mark.

"Well I'm no good in the field, I'm better off staying in the lab," Mark explained.

"I'll remember to leave you there next time," Dorian replied. "Ok help me with her; we'll have to put her in the back seat of my car until she comes round." Mark went over to help Dorian pick up Kate when they heard something behind them breathing heavily; it sounded like a dog... a very big dog. Dorian reached for his gun and quickly turned around to fire at the wolf but it was too quick for him. The wolf jumped up into the tree and climbed up.

"It's getting away!" Mark said.

"Really? I would never have been able to work that out!" Dorian replied bitterly. Mark quickly pulled out his tranquiliser gun and fired at the wolf. The dart hit the wolf on the behind – it howled in pain. "Well done," Dorian said to Mark, "you've managed to piss him off!" The wolf pounced at them but Dorian pulled Mark out of the way.

The wolf landed on the ground and turned to face Dorian and Mark. "Mark," Dorian said, "take Kate back to the car. I'll handle the problem."

Mark slowly walked over to Kate put one of her arms over his shoulder then carried her off to Dorian's car. Dorian on the other hand just stood there and watched the wolf. Suddenly the wolf dived at him but Dorian moved out of the way quickly and fired his tranquiliser gun at the wolf. The dart hit the wolf on the back and Dorian acted quickly; he pulled out his lighter and picked up a stick and set it on fire. The wolf backed away from the fire. "Ha!" Dorian shouted and waved the torch in the wolf's face. It backed away slowly; it was now starting to feel the effects of the tranquiliser. "Steady now," Dorian said to the wolf. It stepped back even further then collapsed to the ground.

With the werewolf asleep, Dorian tied its hands and legs. Mark had returned with rope from Dorian's car. "Why do you have rope in your car boot?" Mark asked Dorian as they began to drag the werewolf to the car.

"It's a long story," Dorian replied.

After what seemed hours but was really only thirty minutes, Dorian and Mark had finally dragged the wolf all the way to Dorian's car. "God this thing's heavy!" Mark panted as he slumped down against the car door.

"I'm getting too old for this," Dorian gasped and collapsed beside Mark.

"How much does that thing weigh?" Mark asked.

"Well," Dorian wheezed, "it's mostly solid muscle so roughly 795 pounds." Mark tried to whistle in amazement but didn't have the breath to do it. "Call, call Dwight and tell him we've, we've caught the werewolf," Dorian panted.

"Get Kate to do it," Mark said.

"You shot her with the tranquiliser, remember?" Dorian told him.

Chapter 13

A Tour of the Underground Headquarters

The wolf was still out cold when they got it back to HQ. Half a dozen armed guards showed up to take it down to isolation and another took Kate down to medics, while Dorian and Mark went to tell Dwight about what had happened.

"You shot Detective Joans!" Dwight said the moment Dorian told him what Mark had done.

"I didn't mean to!" Mark told Dwight, his face red with embarrassment.

"This is the last time I let you go out in the field, Dr Markus," Dwight said firmly, then turned to Dorian. "You were right about this werewolf only recently being bitten. I looked up hospital records from the past week and discovered a boy called Jason Wilson had been taken into hospital after being attacked by some kind of animal. He was kept in for two days then let out the day before yesterday."

"Why hadn't HQ been informed about this boy?" Mark asked both Dorian and Dwight.

"We should have been," Dwight said.

"Then why didn't the agent assigned to watch that hospital send in the report?" Mark asked again.

"Because someone held it back," Dwight explained. "I only got this file in an hour after you called me at the park," he told Dorian. "That's how I found out about this boy," and Dwight held up the hospital report. "Why do I suspect Harfang had something to do with this?" Dwight said to Dorian.

"Because the whole thing stinks of him," Dorian replied and took the report out of Dwight's hand and read it. "Well we have Mr Wilson's address here," Dorian told Dwight and Mark. "Maybe we should drop the boy off home."

"What!" Mark cried. "After all the trouble we've been through, we're just going to let him go!"

"Not entirely," Dwight replied, knowing exactly what Dorian was thinking.

The wolf regained consciousness in the back garden of the house it came from. Slowly it stood up then climbed back up to the opened window and back into the room it came from. It curled up on the bed then went to sleep.

Dorian, Dwight, and Mark watched the wolf go back into the house it came from. "So what now?" Mark asked them both as they crouched back behind the fence.

"We pop by in the morning," Dorian told him.

"And do what?" Mark asked, still not sure of the plan.

"Use your brains, boy," Dwight said. "Vampires

and werewolves don't get along. If we have a werewolf on our side then Harfang may get nervous and make mistakes."

"I doubt he'll make a mistake," Dorian said, "but he will get nervous. Werewolves are the only creatures on this planet that can pick up the scent of vampires."

Jason woke up early the next morning. As he got out of bed his behind felt sore, as if he had just had a flu shot. After getting washed and changed, Jason headed downstairs where his mother was making breakfast. "Morning," she said to him as he sat down at the breakfast table. "Sleep well?" his mum asked as she handed him a bowl of cereal.

"Yeah," Jason lied. He hadn't told her about how he kept turning into a monster at night, she might have thought her son was going crazy. "Rachel called while you were in the bathroom," Mrs Wilson told her son. "She wants to know when you're going back to school."

"I wanted to go back today," Jason replied, frustrated with being stuck in the house twenty-four seven.

"The doctors said you couldn't go back until your wounds are fully healed," his mum explained.

Suddenly the doorbell rang.

"Coming," Mrs Wilson called as she walked over to the front door. Mrs Wilson opened the front door; a handsome man in a blue suit was standing there on the front porch. He had a cane and lovely brown hair. "Can I help you?" Mrs Wilson asked the man in the blue suit.

"Yes I'm Mr Gray, I work for Scotland Yard," the man in the blue suit told her. "I'm here about your son."

"He hasn't done anything wrong," Mrs Wilson told Mr Gray.

"I know that ma'am, I'm here because your son was chosen to do a work experience course at the Yard," Mr Gray explained to Mrs Wilson.

"Are students allowed to do a work experience course at Scotland Yard?" Mrs Wilson asked. It was something she hadn't heard about before and she didn't know if work experience at the Yard was even legally allowed. "Of course they are," Mr Gray said.

"May we come in?" said a woman who had just joined Mr Gray.

"Oh, of course. Mrs Wilson this is Detective Kate Joans," Mr Gray told Mrs Wilson.

"You're walking funny, are you alright?" Mrs Wilson asked Detective Joans.

"I'm fine thank you," Kate replied.

"Do come in," Mrs Wilson said and let Dorian and Kate in and stepped into the dining room where Jason was having breakfast.

"Who are you?" Jason asked.

"I'm Detective Kate Joans," Kate told Jason, and showed him her badge.

"Apparently you were chosen to do a work experience course at Scotland Yard," Jason's mum told him.

"Is that allowed?" Jason asked.

"Has been since 1997," Dorian told Jason and handed Mrs Wilson a letter explaining the work experience at Scotland Yard. "There's a number on the letter if you want to contact someone at Scotland Yard to back me up if you'd like," Dorian told Mrs Wilson.

"I'll do that now," Mrs Wilson replied.

"If it's ok with you Mrs Wilson, we'd like to discuss what Jason will be doing if he chooses to do his work experience with us," Kate said to Mrs Wilson.

"I'll just be in the other room if you need me," Mrs Wilson replied and went to use the phone.

Dorian sat down across from Jason, Kate sat next to him, and they both looked at Jason. "I understand you were attacked by a wolf a few nights back," Kate said to Jason. Jason looked at them both.

"Yes, yes that's right, I didn't know the incident was filed at Scotland Yard," Jason replied.

"We don't work for Scotland Yard, Jason," Dorian told him.

"But she's got a badge," Jason said, pointing at Kate.

"We work with Scotland Yard," Kate explained to Jason. "Whenever something strange or unexplainable happens, the police call us in and we find the answers and the culprits."

Jason looked at them both. "What sort of strange things?" he asked them.

"The supernatural," Dorian replied. "Like a sixteen-year-old boy who gets bitten by a wolf and turns into a werewolf a few days after he's bitten, turning said boy into a lethal killing machine." Dorian looked at Jason, who looked at them both, scared.

"How, how did you know what happened to me?" he asked them both, slightly scared.

"We have your hospital records, Jason," Kate told him. "We also took blood samples from a werewolf we caught last night," she said. "They match the blood samples taken from you when you were in hospital, Jason."

Jason went silent.

"I really did kill someone, didn't I?" Jason said to them both.

"I'm afraid so, Jason," Dorian replied sadly.

"My mum can't find out about this," Jason told them both.

"We understand, Jason," Kate said, looking at him as though she truly did know how he felt, "which is why we're going to make you an offer."

Jason looked at them. "What kind of offer?" he asked.

"We're working a case and we need a werewolf to help us with the investigation. If you help us we can give you medication to help you with your problem," Dorian explained.

"And you won't give me the medication unless I help you?" Jason said.

"No, we'll get you the medication whether you help us or not, but if you did help us, we could make sure this problem of yours can never interfere with your future life," Dorian told Jason. "By offering you a job."

Dorian and Kate left after Mrs Wilson came back from talking on the phone. She said that Scotland Yard confirmed Dorian's story and that she would be happy to let Jason start the work experience tomorrow. Jason sat on his bed, reading. Kate had given Jason some of the tablets to stop him from turning into that monster tonight and he took two the moment they left. He thought about what his future might be like now that he turned into a seven foot tall wolf-like monster nearly every night, but Mr Gray and Detective Joans had given him hope of a future once again.

When Jason came downstairs the next morning, Kate was already there. "Ready?" Kate asked him as he entered the kitchen. Mrs Wilson had gotten Kate a cup of coffee.

"Yes," Jason replied.

"Good," Kate said, and put her mug down and got up. "Thank you for the coffee Mrs Wilson," Kate said. "I'll be sure to bring him back before his bed time," Kate told Jason's mum.

"I don't have a bed time," Jason said to Kate as they headed for the door.

"It's ten thirty," his mum told Kate.

"Mum!" Jason put on his shoes, grabbed his coat and followed Kate out the door.

"Sleep well?" Kate asked Jason as they walked to her car.

"Yes, those tablets worked, thank you," Jason told her. They got into the car and set off into London.

"Who was that guy you were with yesterday?" Jason asked Kate as they drove past some shops.

"Dorian Gray," Kate replied.

Jason looked at her. "As in the fictional character created by Oscar Wilde?" he said.

"Yes," she replied.

"The guy who sold his soul to the devil so he would stay forever young and his painting would age instead of him!" Jason went on.

"The same," Kate said.

"But he's fictional, and even if he was real, he lived in 1890 and died in the same time and era."

"Dracula died and came back on more than one occasion," Kate told him.

"He doesn't exist either," Jason said firmly.

"Kid, you have a lot to learn," Kate said.

They arrived at an old abandoned car park next to an old subway station. "Where exactly are we going?" Jason asked Kate as they got out of the car.

"To where I work," Kate said, and handed him a visitor badge. "You'll need that," she told him, and they got out of the car and walked towards an elevator. They stepped inside the elevator and Kate pressed the down button.

"Where exactly do you work again?" Jason asked Kate as the elevator began to descend.

"It's sort of kept a secret from the public," Kate told him.

"Why?"

"Because if the public found out they might think we were crazy."

Jason was starting to have doubts about this. They soon stopped at what felt like far underground. When they stepped out, Jason found to his surprise they were in a well-lit circular room with a marble floor and a huge rug in the centre; there were two more elevators in the room, both on either side of the one Jason and Kate had come in. On the left-hand side of the room was a door that led off down one corridor, and on the right-hand side was another door. Ahead of them both was a huge archway that led to an even bigger library with the sign above the arch calling the library 'The Hall of Records', and in front of the arch was a bronze statue of a man wearing a Victorian suit. He had sleek hair, eyes that even as a statue beamed with vast intellect, and a face that suggested the man might have been in his late forties, early fifties. In his right hand was a cross and in the other was what appeared to be a wooden stake, and the plaque on the base of the statue said: 'Abraham Van Helsing: science professor, vampire hunter, and one of five founders of the Underground, now known as HQ'.

"Where are we?" Jason asked as he looked around the room.

"We call it HQ," Kate explained. "C'mon," she said, and they headed for the arch.

Jason couldn't believe his eyes when he saw the library. It must have been nearly three floors high, shelves full of books stacked in nearly every order possible; in the centre of the library were rows of tables where people could sit and read the book they'd picked, there were even a few old fashion leather sofas and armchairs too. They exited through a smaller arch in the far, far corner of the Hall of Records and walked down a long corridor where people were walking in and out of rooms carrying files and reports. They took a turn and walked down another corridor where two people were hanging up a painting of a man with a beard and smoking a cigar. "Is that Bram Stoker?" Jason asked Kate, pointing to the picture.

"Yes, he was one of the founders of this establishment," she explained to Jason. "There was him, Professor Van Helsing, Robert Louis Stevenson, Mary Shelly, and Washington Irving."

Jason was amazed. "Van Helsing really existed!" he said in amazement.

"So did Doctor Victor Frankenstein, and the Invisible Man, but know one's seen him in years," Kate said.

They soon arrived at the office of Richard Dwight, Caretaker of HQ. When they stepped into his office, Dwight stood up. "The great Jason! You have no idea how much bloody trouble you've caused us," Dwight said, smiling as he shook Jason's hand. "You've already meet Dorian I assume." Dwight gestured to Dorian, who was standing in the corner drinking coffee. "I imagine you have a lot of questions you want to ask about this place," Dwight said to Jason as he sat down.

"Yes actually," Jason said as he sat down. "How can the people who write the novels such as Dracula and Frankenstein exist if their characters do?" Jason asked them all.

"Ah, well that's rather simple really," Dwight explained. "The events in these books really did happen and the authors were involved in some of these events. When they published these stories they just removed any part they played in the event, otherwise people might have thought them mad."

"So what exactly is this place?" Jason asked Dwight.

"This is the Underground, but we just call it HQ these days," Dwight said as he poured himself another cup of coffee. "We handle cases more in depth than the police, such as a vampire attack, invisible men, or werewolf killings," he explained.

"This place was founded in 1850 by four of the greatest writers of all time, Bram Stoker, Mary Shelly, Robert Louis Stevenson, and Washington Irving. They used to meet at a pub to discuss the supernatural, such as vampires, mummies, and the living dead; Irving had an obsession with headless people though. Anyway, they called their little group the Underground and began research into these creatures, and Mary Shelly had proposed they learn ways to fight these creatures through science, in the memory of her friend Victor Frankenstein. Thirty-seven years passed and in 1887, Bram Stoker was visiting a friend of his in Whitby. His friend was Doctor Jack Seward, who was currently dealing with one of his most baffling cases yet – a young woman named Lucy Westenra who had become ill of late and had lost a lot of blood. It was around this time Seward called for the help of his old friend Professor Abraham Van Helsing. He quickly discovered that it was a vampire behind the suffering of Miss Lucy, but he was too late to do anything. That vampire's name was Count Dracula. With the help of Bram Stoker and a Mister Johnathan Harker, Van Helsing was able to vanquish Dracula and destroy him."

"So the stories are true!" Jason said at last, after taking in everything Dwight had told him.

"Van Helsing agreed to help form the Underground as an expert in fending off vampires and the Hunters were formed," Dwight said.

"What are Hunters?"

"They hunt down and capture or arrest any rogue vampires or werewolves, and if necessary, kill them if they have no other choice and the lives of innocent people are at risk. Now to business, the reason we brought you here, Mr Wilson, is because we're currently working on a case that involves a vampire," Dwight explained, and Dorian handed Jason a file. Jason opened the file; inside was a picture of a man with pale skin and white hair and he wore a black suit.

"This is Amadeus Harfang, a criminal vampire who has evaded capture for one hundred and fifty years now. He recently came to England and has already killed a woman. We don't know what he's up to and he was behind the werewolf attack that got you bitten, I'm afraid," Dorian told Jason.

"What do you need me for exactly?" Jason asked them all.

"Werewolves and vampires have never truly had a friendly relationship, in fact werewolves can sniff out a vampire from sixty feet away, and you may not know it yet, but as you carry on becoming a werewolf, you'll learn to hate Harfang as much as the next werewolf. It's in your instincts to hate him," Dorian explained.

"Well with that said and done, Joans, why don't you show Mr Jason around?" Dwight said to Kate, and they both left the room.

"What do you think?" Dwight asked Dorian.

"He's young, inexperienced, and unsure with what do with his life now that it's changed," Dorian replied as they watched Jason and Kate walk down the corridor.

Kate took Jason down to evidence storage first. It was a large room with hundreds of rows of shelves filled with boxes and labelled translucent bags with stuff inside them. "This is evidence storage," Kate explained. "Whenever we close a case all the evidence is stored here in case it's ever needed in court or if we ever need to use the evidence again on a related case."

"Is this really one of Jack the Ripper's knives?" Jason asked, looking at a knife in a glass case which had the sign on top that said 'Jack the Ripper's knife, one of six'.

"Yes," Kate said. "It was discovered at one of the Ripper victim's crime scenes. Scotland Yard sent it here after the case was dropped in 1889, it was just never revealed to the newspapers," Kate told him.

"How much stuff is stored here?" Jason asked Kate, looking around the room.

"Hard to say, we've been storing this stuff since 1887."

They left the storage room and went to the forensic labs where Mark was running tests on soil.

"This is one of our many forensic labs," Kate told Jason as they entered the lab, "and this is Doctor Mark Barker, one of our doctors that work here."

Mark shook Jason's hand. "I mostly work in the morgue," Mark said.

"What are you doing in here anyway?" Kate asked Mark.

"I found traces of soil on the bottom of the victim's shoes," Mark explained, "and considering she comes from another country, this soil may be able to tell us where Harfang's been these past few years and what he's up to."

"Well we know he came here from Bulgaria," Kate said.

"But maybe this soil will tell us whereabouts in the country he was living," Mark replied.

"We'll leave you to do that, I have a few more places to show Jason," Kate told Mark.

"Okay, I'll let you know when I've found something."

"Thanks Mark."

Kate and Jason left forensics and went back to the Hall of Records.

"Have you thought about what you wanted to do when you leave school?" Kate asked Jason as they walked down the Undead aisle.

"Not really," Jason admitted. "I guess there's not a lot I can do now that I'm a, well... unnatural."

"What you are isn't unnatural, Jason," Kate said as they stopped at the Romero section of the aisle.

"Jason, werewolfism isn't unnatural. It makes you different, yes, but not unnatural. It's the same as autism – there are weird and frightening things about autism but it's not unnatural, it makes you who you are. There is no truly natural person in the world, the only thing there is are people, people with different lives, different hobbies, different friends, and that's one of the things that makes us who we are. We're all different."

Jason was about to reply when Dorian popped his head round the corner. "Thought you two would be in here. Mark's found something, c'mon," he told Jason and Kate. They both followed Dorian out of the library and back down to forensics. Mark was stood next to a computer with a file in his hand.

"Turns out Harfang wasn't living in Bulgaria, he was hiding just outside Switzerland. The soil on Mary Creed's shoes confirmed that," Mark explained to them all and handed over the file for all three of them to look at. "Dwight said he'll have someone check up on where Harfang was living and see if there's any evidence as to what he's doing here," Mark said.

"Maybe someone realised he was living in Switzerland and he had to leave and hide in Britain," Jason suggested.

"Not a bad idea," Dorian said as he read the file, "but this is the capital for Hunters all over the world, for Harfang to come here would be like walking straight into the lion's den."

"What did this Marry Creed do before she died?" Jason asked Mark.

"Well according to these files we got from

Switzerland she was a historian and archaeologist. She wrote a paper on Vlad the Impaler and studied the Roman Empire and vampirism."

"What!" Kate said, looking at Marry Creed's file.

"Maybe that's why Harfang killed her," Mark told Kate. "She found out he was a vampire and was going to call the Switzerland branch of the Underground."

"I think we need to pay another visit to Harfang's," Dorian said to Kate.

"Dwight will kill you if you do," Mark said to Dorian.

"I'm immortal remember?" Dorian replied and headed for the door.

"Hang on," Jason said as he looked at Marry Creed's file. "Her name's familiar," he told Kate and the others.

"She studied vampirism, maybe you saw one of her books in the Hall of Records," Kate said to him.

"We don't have any books by Marry Creed in the Hall of Records," Mark informed Kate.

"Then where have you heard the name from?" Dorian asked Jason curiously.

"It was at the Natural History Museum when I went on a school trip two months ago. She and some other archaeologists were having an exhibit opened up for something they'd just discovered," Jason explained.

"What was it?" Dorian asked.

"I can't remember," Jason confessed.

"Right, Kate, you and Jason go down to the museum and find out what exhibit the museum was going to open. I'll stay here and find out what Creed and her colleagues discovered," Dorian told Kate.

"What about me?" Mark asked Dorian.

"Stay here and try not to shoot any more people in the ass," Kate told Mark and left the lab.

"What did she mean by that?" Jason asked Dorian.

"It's a long story," Dorian replied, and Jason rushed after Kate.

Chapter 14

Field Trip

Jason and Kate arrived at the Natural History Museum shortly after two in the afternoon. They parked across the street from the museum and ran across to the front doors. "Where did you see this sign?" Kate asked Jason as they entered the museum and walked up the marble stairs.

"Down here," Jason told her, and they walked down a long corridor full of medieval stuff. They soon arrived at an area of the museum that had been boarded off and closed for construction and furnishing, and a sign that said 'Coming soon, new ground breaking discovery in archaeology. Discovered in Israel by archaeologists Eric Morgan, Jessica Bates, Thomas Harrison and Marry Creed'. "I know these people," Jason said. Kate looked at him. "They're famous in the historical society, Professor Morgan and Doctor Bates are experts in religious studies, particularly in Jesus and his crucifixion," Jason explained to Kate. "About three years ago, they found a cross that might have come from the hill where Jesus is supposed to have been crucified."

"I remember hearing about that," Kate said,

"apparently it caused a lot of arguments in the science community. So who's this Thomas Harrison?" Kate asked Jason.

"I only really know about his books on the Roman Empire," Jason replied.

"So he's an expert on Roman history too, like Marry Creed," Kate said.

"Yes," Jason admitted. "So, Roman historians and experts in religious studies went to Israel on an expedition together, but what did they go looking for?" Jason said. "Whatever it is, it must be worth keeping a secret to the public until it goes on display."

Kate got out her phone. "Dwight might know someone who can tell us what they found in Israel," she told Jason, and went to stand in a corner as she made the call.

Dorian was on a computer in the Hall of Records trying the find out what Creed had discovered on the expedition when Dwight walked up to him. "I just got a call from Kate," Dwight told him. "Apparently Marry Creed went on an expedition to Israel with three other people, a professor and two doctors," he explained.

"Damn it!" Dorian said, hitting the side of the computer. "The damn thing won't work again."

"You weren't made for the microchip era, were you?" Dwight said to Dorian.

"I was born in 1870, remember?" Dorian said, annoyed.

"Excuse me Mr Gray." A woman approached Dorian and Dwight. "This just arrived for you," she said, and handed him an A4 envelope.

"Who delivered it?" Dwight asked the woman as Dorian opened the envelope.

"A man came to the front desk and handed it in, sir," the woman told Dwight.

"Oh no," Dorian said as he dropped the envelope.

"What's wrong?" Dwight asked.

"Look," Dorian replied, and handed him a picture. It was of Kate when she had left her apartment that morning to go and pick up Jason. There was a note. Dwight read it. "You know what happens to people who dig to deep, Gray," he read. "Harfang's going to have Kate killed!" Dorian told him as he put his coat on.

"I'll try and get in contact with her, you just get to the museum as fast as you can!" Dwight said. "You might want to send some backup," Dorian said as he ran out the Hall of Records, hoping he wasn't too late.

Crown and his zombies entered the museum and no one suspected them as they walked in; the fluid Harfang had given them helped them blend in with crowds, even though shopping people looked like zombies already. Crown turned to the four zombies who followed him. "Harfang wants Dorian's detective friend dead, you know what to do," he told them, and they went upstairs.

Kate was still trying to get hold of HQ; Jason was leaning against the archway when he noticed someone at the bottom of the corridor. "Finally," Kate said as her phone started ringing. "Hello, sir..." Kate said but

Dwight cut her off.

"Harfang has sent his people out to kill you, get back here now!"

Suddenly Jason pulled Kate to the floor as someone shot at them. "Thanks," Kate said as she looked up at Jason.

"Who are they?" Jason asked her as they crawled over to the other arch. "Zombies," Kate told him.

"They don't look like any zombies I've ever seen," Jason said as they got up and ran down the corridor.

"They take a special drug that makes them more human than zombie," she explained as they ran down an art corridor. Suddenly there came more shots that luckily missed them both; Kate quickly got out her gun and fired back at their attackers but missed.

"How many were there?" Jason asked as they turned down another corridor full of people.

"Two," Kate replied, then got out her badge. "Police, everyone stay calm, I need you all to leave the building now!" she shouted, just as two more shots were fired by a zombie. The people didn't argue with Kate and ran for the nearest way out. "C'mon," Kate said to Jason.

Dorian pulled up outside the museum. People were running out. He grabbed his walking stick and ran for the door. Suddenly he heard someone shooting inside the building; he ran as fast as he could and prayed to God he wasn't too late.

Kate and Jason ran down into a room full of animals that had been stuffed and mounted. "We've got to try and get back downstairs," Kate told Jason as they crouched behind a display of stuffed tigers.

Suddenly, they heard someone enter the room. "I saw them head in this direction," said one of the zombies, as another followed him into the room.

"Remember, Harfang wants them dead," said the other zombie.

"Ask Harfang what it's like to want," Kate said and jumped up and shot one of the zombies in the head and it dropped to the floor, then she shot the other in the shoulder and he dropped the gun.

"Jason, get his gun," Kate told Jason. Jason did as she asked and went over to the zombie and took his gun. "Now tell me what Harfang's up to!" Kate said to the zombie.

"Do you think I'm stupid?" the zombie asked Kate.

"Considering you tried to kill me I'd say yeah," Kate replied and handcuffed the zombie. "I'm sure one of the Hunters back at HQ can make you talk," she told the zombie, and the three walked out of the room.

Dorian entered the museum as more people ran past him. He looked up at the top of the stairs and saw Crown. "Crown!" he yelled as he ran towards him. Crown pulled out his gun and shot Dorian down.

"You have no idea how long I've waited to shoot you," Crown said as he walked down to Dorian.

Suddenly Dorian got up and kicked the gun out of Crown's hand and got out his sword quickly and held it at Crown's throat. "What have you done to Kate and the boy?" Dorian asked angrily.

"They're probably dead now," Crown told Dorian.

"If they are then you better hope Harfang knows how to stitch you back together!" Dorian said. Suddenly, without warning, Dorian stabbed his sword into Crown's left foot.

"Arrr!" Crown yelled in pain. Suddenly two more zombies showed up from down a corridor. Dorian snatched Crown's gun and shot one of them in the head, the other was about to fire at Dorian when he was shot through the head from behind. Kate and Jason arrived in the entrance hall with a zombie in cuffs.

"Dwight got in touch with you then," Dorian said, relieved.

"We were able to get this," Kate said, nodding towards the cuffed zombie. "We'll take him back to HQ and interrogate him, he might know what Harfang is up to."

"No," Dorian said. "He's a foot soldier, Harfang wouldn't tell him anything, but Crown here might know something." Dorian got out a pair of handcuffs and put them on Crown. "Let him go," Dorian said to Kate, nodding to the zombie in cuffs. "I want you to tell Harfang that he failed to kill my partner, and also tell him we have his friend in custody," Dorian told the zombie. He nodded then ran out of the museum. "Take him in, Kate," Dorian said as he headed for the door.

"Where are you going?" Jason asked Dorian.

"To get a drink," Dorian replied, and left the museum.

Kate dropped Jason back off at home after they took Crown to HQ. His mum was waiting for him in the kitchen. "Sorry I'm late home," Jason said to his mum as he poured himself some orange juice.

"It's alright," his mum replied. "Your sister called while you were out. She wanted to know how you were," she told him.

"I'm doing fine," Jason replied.

Suddenly he felt sick.

"Are you alright?" his mum asked as she walked over to him.

"Bathroom!" Jason said quickly and rushed upstairs as fast as he could; he ran into the bathroom and shut the door behind him. Jason knelt over the toilet and threw up. Jason leaned back after he was sick and rested his head against the bathroom wall; he looked into the toilet and saw what looked like human flesh in his vomit, along with what looked like the remains of a person's liver. He must have eaten them the other night when he first turned into a werewolf. The thought of eating a person's organs made Jason sick again.

"Are you alright in there?" Jason's mum asked from outside the bathroom.

"I was sick," Jason admitted, but didn't tell his mum about the liver in his vomit or the flesh.

"Do you want me to call Detective Joan and tell her you can't go in tomorrow?" she asked him.

"No, I'll be fine," Jason said.

"Ok," his mum replied. "Brush your teeth then go lay down," she told him, then went back downstairs.

Jason flushed the toilet and brushed his teeth, then went to lie on his bed; he had to talk to someone. He needed to talk to Dorian and Kate about this.

Chapter 15

Two Friends in a Bar

The Northern Star is a pub that is located in the west end of London. Dorian used to visit this pub frequently when he first became immortal; it was where he met his first wife and was where Dorian spent most of his free time now when he wasn't working on a case. He was sat at a table in the far corner drinking red wine. He liked fine wine and considered himself an expert. He was about to order another bottle when Dwight came in and sat down next to him. "How did you know I'd be here?" Dorian asked Dwight.

"Because it's where I first met you," Dwight told him. "You got into a fight with two big lads who probably would have beaten the shit out of you if I hadn't intervened."

"Was I drunk that night?" Dorian asked Dwight, unsure.

"No but you did get a bloody nose from one of those men," Dwight said.

"Good times," Dorian replied, smiling.

"Are we going to have a proper drink or what?"

Dwight asked as he put the half empty bottle of red wine to one side.

"Did Crown tell you anything?" Dorian asked.

"Not yet," Dwight told him. "He's refusing to speak but I was able to get in contact with one of our agents in Switzerland. There wasn't much in Marry Creed's apartment, Harfang must have cleared out every bit of information she had from her expedition. All they were able to find was a map of Israel and this picture." Dwight handed Dorian a picture of Jesus' crucifixion. Dorian had seen this picture before at HQ but couldn't remember where.

"Have you ever seen this particular image of the crucifixion before?" Dorian asked Dwight.

"Probably, but it must have been years ago," he said to Dorian. "We'll probably know more tomorrow when we interrogate Crown," Dwight told Dorian.

"You're right" Dorian said as he got up.

"Going already?" Dwight said, amazed.

"I really don't want to be hung over when we interrogate him tomorrow," Dorian replied as he put on his coat. "Dwight, could you get someone to look for this picture in the Hall of Records? I'm sure I've seen it somewhere before," Dorian said. "I'll get Mr Wilson on it tomorrow morning when he comes in with Kate," Dwight replied, and Dorian left the pub.

Chapter 16

The Interrogation

Kate picked up Jason at ten forty-five the next morning and they made their way back to HQ. "How are you feeling today?" Kate asked Jason as they drove past his street.

"Not too well," Jason said. "I was sick last night and I threw up remains of a person's liver," he explained.

"That's probably from when you turned into a werewolf a few nights back. You're not used to having another side to you Jason, but I'd probably let one of the doctors at HQ check you out. Being sick might be a side-effect of the medication you were given for Werewolfism," she told him and they carried on driving down the road.

When they arrived in the car park, Dorian came out to meet them. "We're going to interrogate Crown," he told Kate as they walked towards the elevator.

"Good," Kate said, "with any luck we'll find out what Harfang's up to."

"Hang on," Jason said as they passed a pillar.

"What's wrong?" Kate asked him.

"Get down!" he yelled, and just as he finished saying that, someone drove past, shooting at the three of them. They dropped to the ground fast as the people in the car kept shooting at them.

"Sounds like they're using AK-47s," Kate told Dorian.

"How the hell did they know where to find us?" Jason asked them both.

Suddenly security arrived and started firing at the people in the black car. Dorian quickly got up and start shooting back at the people in the car. "Great, it's more zombies," he told Kate as she got out her gun.

"Does Harfang know where this place is?" Jason asked Dorian.

"Know about it? He was around when it was first built," Dorian told him.

The car soon drove off but Dorian and Kate were able to kill at least two of the zombies but in return, they had wounded three of the security guards. "Call Mark and tell him we have three men who need medical attention now," Dorian told Kate, and she quickly got out her phone.

Things had become hectic in HQ after the attack in the car park; medics were rushing around, security was everywhere, and Dwight was in the centre of the main hall in front of Van Helsing's statue shouting orders around. "I want security in the car park doubled!" he said to one security officer. "And check security cameras, they may be able to tell us which way the attackers went when they escaped," he told another.

"Harfang must not want us to interrogate Crown," Kate said to Dorian as they headed off towards the interrogation room.

"Obviously," Dorian replied as they came to the door. "You can go into the other room and watch," Dorian told Jason. "Crown was a Nazi and an old acquaintance of mine," he said.

"What do you mean by acquaintance?" Jason asked.

"I killed him," Dorian replied and stepped into the interrogation room, and Kate followed him in. Jason was about to go into the other room to watch when Dwight caught up with him.

"Wilson, I need you to do something for me," he said as he walked up to Jason. "We got this picture from one of our agents in Switzerland, it was found in the victim's apartment but Dorian and I think we've seen it somewhere before. Could you go into the Hall of Records and see what you can find out about it?"

"Yes sir," Jason said, and walked off with the picture down to the Hall of Records.

Dorian and Kate stepped into the interrogation room. Crown was sat at a table with his hands cuffed. "Morning Crown, I trust you slept well," Dorian said to Crown as he and Kate sat down.

"You have quite the history, Mr Crown," Kate said as she looked at his file. "Wanted for war crimes, weapons smuggling, and murder, but I guess that's what you expect from someone who works for

Amadeus Harfang."

"I don't work for Harfang," Crown said. "I've never even heard the name."

"Well that's a lie since everywhere he goes you go and you've known him since 1943," Dorian replied.

Crown looked at Dorian menacingly. "You're still chasing him after all these years, Dorian. If Van Helsing couldn't get him, what makes you think you can?" Crown asked Dorian harshly.

"Because we have a werewolf working with us now," Dorian said smoothly, "and we both know vampires and werewolves don't get on well," he told Crown. Crown leaned back in his chair, trying not to look worried.

"What's Harfang up to?" Kate asked Crown. He looked at her and smiled.

"How should I know?" he asked her.

"You're his right-hand man," Dorian said back.

"Maybe, but he doesn't tell me everything," Crown replied. Dorian was starting to lose his patience with him.

"Well, what do you know?" Kate asked him firmly.

"Only that he's planning something big," Crown said, "something that will leave an everlasting impression on this country and the rest of the world in history."

Dorian and Kate looked at one another.

"How does Marry Creed fit into all of this?"

"Look Detective, I never even heard of that

woman until Harfang became obsessed with her, I didn't even know what she did for a living until Harfang told us to clear out her apartment," Crown told Kate.

Dorian got up and walked away. "Your English is improving, Crown," was all he said before he left the room, and Kate followed him out.

"What do you think?" Kate asked Dwight as they walked out of the interrogation room.

"I don't believe him," Dwight said.

"Me neither," Dorian admitted. "He knows more than he's telling us, we may have to consider truth serum," he told Dwight and Kate.

"Harfang knows our methods, he probably gave his zombies something to counteract it," Kate told them.

"She's right," Dwight said as they walked down the corridor. "I say we wait until we find out where Creed went on her expedition and see if it gives us any clues as to what Harfang's up to, and see how Crown reacts when we tell him."

"Good idea," Dorian replied. "We should probably see if Jason's found anything."

Chapter 17

Kisses and Silver

Jason was examining the picture of Jesus in the Hall of Records; he was trying to find the name of the artist on it or even the artist's signature. If he could find that then he might be able to find out if the picture was published in any books. Sure enough, Jason found the artist's signature – a C. Francis. Jason logged onto one of the computers and searched for Francis's work on the internet.

He discovered that Francis had had his work published in several different religious illustrated books and four other different books, but the picture he had could be found in a book in the vampire section. So Jason wrote down the name of the book and went off to look for it. He walked down the vampire section, examining the spines of the books and their titles. Jason had no idea that there had been so many books published on the study and history of vampires, of course Bram Stoker's novel was in among them, but he didn't see a single Twilight book in this library; Rachel probably wouldn't have liked it here. Finally, Jason found the book he was looking for, it was a big, heavy, black hardback book titled *The First: The Origin and Legacy of the Vampires*. It had been written by an Edgar Val-Joan. Jason took the book back to his table and began searching for the page that had the picture of Jesus' crucifixion.

Dorian, Kate, and Dwight soon arrived in the Hall of Records. They walked past a bunch of people reading up on the experiments and research of a famous scientist from Germany and came to where Jason was sat, reading an old black book. "Found anything?" Kate asked him as she sat beside him.

"Yes, actually," Jason told them as he turned a page in the book. "The picture your agents found, Mr Dwight, was a picture used in this book," Jason informed Dwight.

"Which book is that?" Dwight asked.

"It's about the origin of vampires and it tells the story about how Judas betrayed Jesus to the Roman soldiers, and goes on to tell how after Jesus was crucified, Judas committed suicide by hanging himself as punishment for his betrayal of Jesus. God cursed Judas into an undead state, forcing him to feed off the blood of the living and hiding in the shadows away from the sun, making Judas the first vampire," Jason explained to everyone.

"Impressive," Dorian said. He had heard this story a million times. "But what does this have to do with Creed and whatever Harfang's up to?"

"Look closely at the picture," Jason advised. Dorian picked up the picture and examined it closely, he could see a Roman officer handing what looks like a bag of money to Judas.

"Is that supposed to be Judas?" Dorian said. "And is that the thirty pieces Judas was given for betraying

Jesus?"

"Thirty pieces of silver, to be precise," Jason replied. "And if you remember the tale, those thirty pieces were seen as a sin towards God and are the reason vampires are vulnerable to silver, however these thirty pieces were melted down and were made into a cup, a chalice to be correct..."

"The Judas Chalice," Dorian finished off. "The vampire version of the Holy Grail."

"My god, Dorian do you realise what would happen if Harfang got his hands on it?" Dwight said.

"Well it has the ability to raise vampires back from the dead," Jason told them. "I mean, well, they're already dead but..."

"I know what you meant," Kate said to Jason.

"But are there many deceased vampires in Britain?" Jason asked them.

"You have no idea," Kate replied. "Whitby has the highest number of deceased vampires, it's where we send any criminal vampires, after they die from natural causes that kill vampires, or are murdered, or even died in prison," she explained to Jason.

"And if Harfang brings them back to life they will be under his control, then all hell will break loose," Dwight said as he got out his phone.

"We need to find out if this was what Creed went on the expedition for, to find the Chalice. If it has been found then we need to know, and now." Dwight left the Hall of Records.

Dorian looked at Kate and Jason seriously. "The Judas Chalice can do more than raise the dead, it can hypnotise and control other vampires nearby," he told them both, and got up to follow Dwight out of the library. "Good job finding this information out, Jason," he said as he left. "You'll make a great detective someday."

Dwight was able to get through to some contacts of his and was able to pull some strings; Dorian was down in the training room, practicing his fencing, and Jason and Kate were in the Hall of Records trying to find more information on the Judas Chalice. "I had no idea there were so many books on the Chalice," Jason admitted as they took down four more books from the top shelves.

"We have an entire section of the library for the Judas Chalice," Kate said as they climbed down the ladders. They returned to their table and began looking through more books, when Dwight came in with three other men carrying computer parts.

"I was able to get in contact with some colleagues in Switzerland. One of them founded the expedition to Israel and was able to get in contact with the other members of the expedition, and he has had what information Marry Creed had on the Chalice sent to us immediately," Dwight told them as the men began setting up the computer. "Fortunately all her work was on this computer she used while in Israel."

"Where's Dorian?" Kate asked as she looked around the room.

"He's down in one of the training rooms," Dwight said. "Jason, he should be in the training room directly below us, go down there and tell him we have more information."

"Yes sir," Jason replied, and left the Hall of Records.

He took the elevator down to the training room, it looked like the sports hall at Jason's school – a wooden tiled floor with beige-coloured walls, but they had target boards in this room, something they didn't have at Jason's school, along with crossbows, arrows, swords and even one or two axes. "Move back," Dorian said. Jason quickly stepped back and seconds later an arrow flew past and hit the centre of the target board.

"That was amazing," Jason said, impressed.

"Not really," Dorian said as he got another arrow, "it's just the result of practice over a long period of time," he told Jason and handed him the crossbow. "You try."

"No, I'm not that good with any form of weapon," Jason explained to Dorian.

"Look, Jason, if you're going to be working with us here at HQ, then you're going to have to learn to defend yourself." Hesitantly, Jason picked up the crossbow. "Point it at your target and aim," Dorian instructed. Jason did as he was told. "Now focus on your target, concentrate, concentrate, and fire." Jason fired but failed to hit the board in the centre. "Not bad, but I've seen better," Dorian admitted.

"So have I," Jason replied. "Dwight has got some more information for us," he told Dorian.

"Excellent, I'll come now," Dorian said, and put his coat back on.

They arrived back in the Hall of Records. Creed's

computer was set up and Kate was sat at it trying to unlock the user protection on the computer. "Problems?" Dorian asked as he and Jason approached them.

"The computer's password protected," Kate said, "and this particular computer was used by all four scientists in Israel, so each had a different user's document and a different password," she explained.

"Have you tried looking for fingerprints on the keyboard to see which letters they used?" Jason asked.

"We have," Dwight replied, "but the trouble is half of them used some of the same letters in their passwords so we can't make out which are Marry Creed's fingerprints."

"Let me have a look," Jason said, and Kate got up out of the chair and let Jason sit down. Kate picked up the UV light and shone it onto the keyboard and various fingerprints appeared "See what we mean?" Kate said, but Jason looked at the keyboard closely.

"It's kiss," he told them.

"What?" Dorian asked.

"The password is kiss" Jason said again, and started typing the word.

"Creed studied religion history and a kiss was how Judas sold Jesus out to the Romans, by sealing his fate with a kiss," he explained, and the computer allowed them access to Creed's files.

"That was bloody brilliant Wilson," Dwight said, amazed.

Jason found all of Marry Creed's files on the computer. "Which one shall we look at first?" Kate asked Dorian.

"We'll print them all off and we'll all take one to read," Dorian told them all.

"Good idea," Dwight replied.

Half an hour later, they were all sat around a table reading the files. Dwight had got Mark out of his lab to come and help them look through the files. "Half of these notes aren't even written in English," Mark said as he flicked through one of the files.

"We're going to have to scan them into the computer and have them translated," Kate told them as she picked up another file.

"I think I've found something," Dwight said. Everyone looked at him. "On March 16th 2012, the team explored the ruins of a cave not far from the rumoured location of where Jesus was crucified. Inside the cave, they discovered the remains of a burial chamber; the tomb was empty but beneath the tomb they discovered a chest, and inside the chest were scrolls and parchment telling the story of Judas and his betrayal…"

"They actually found Judas's tomb!" Jason gasped.

"That's not all," Dwight said. "By March 20th they had fully examined every inch of the cave and found something else, the Judas Chalice," Dwight read.

"What!" Mark said, shocked. "But, but that's impossible, people have been searching for it for years and found nothing. How did they find it?"

"Well according to this it was by complete accident that they found it," Dwight explained. "Jessica Bates cut her hand on an ancient dagger and the blood from her hand landed on a stone tile of Judas's face, and the blood ran down to the mouth and the mouth opened up, and the Chalice was inside." Everyone went silent.

"When does the Chalice arrive here?" Dorian asked, breaking the silence.

"On the 22nd of October," Dwight read off one of the files.

"That's tomorrow," Kate replied.

"Do we know what airport it will be arriving at?" Mark asked Dwight.

"No but I can contact the other members of the expedition; they've already been told that Creed's been killed, they don't know it was a vampire that killed her though and that's how I want to keep it," Dwight said as he got up and left the library.

"We need to get the Chalice before Harfang does when it arrives tomorrow," Dorian told the other three.

"I can't help you with that tomorrow," Jason said to them. "I have to go back to school tomorrow and I have a test."

"Okay," Dorian replied. "I'll ask Dwight to post two Hunters outside the school on watch in case Harfang comes after you, the zombie we let leave the museum must have told him we'd brought you in to help us."

Kate dropped Jason back off at home a little after six. After he had dinner with his mum, Jason had gone upstairs to do some revision for his test tomorrow, but all he could think about was the

Chalice's arrival into the country tomorrow and how much damage it might cause in the wrong hands, and how much the world he'd known was changing; he had been dragged into another world he didn't even know existed, and now he was caught in the middle of both worlds.

Chapter 18

Methods of Death

The news of Crown's arrest came as a blow to Harfang. Crown knew everything that Harfang had planned, but he knew Crown. He wouldn't give any information to the Hunters; he trusted him but when he got word that a werewolf was helping Dorian Gray on this case, he knew he had to do something. His werewolf plan to distract Dorian had backfired and now this boy was a threat and had to be dealt with.

Harfang had found out that the boy went to Milson Secondary School and he would be there tomorrow. "I want the boy dead," Harfang told his zombies. "Tomorrow, he'll be at the school and no one from the Underground will be there to save him."

"How should we deal with him?" one of the zombies asked Harfang.

"Use your imagination," Harfang replied, smiling.

Chapter 19

Attack on the School

Jason arrived at school at the usual time. He said hello to a few of the boys in his maths class then headed for English.

Rachel had saved him a seat next to her at the back of the classroom. "How are you feeling?" Rachel asked him as he sat down next to her.

"I'm feeling better than I was before," he said. He was told not to tell anyone about HQ, not that anyone would believe him, but Jason didn't want to get Rachel involved and put her in harm's way like he had been at the museum the other day.

Miss Carlson walked into the class room and placed her folder down on her desk. "Quiet," she said, as she got out her whiteboard pen to write on the board. She was new to the school and had only started working there four months ago. "Now as you all know, we have a test today and I'd appreciate it if everyone did it in silence." There was something about Miss Carlson that gave her the ability to get everyone's attention and do as she asked in class. The class went silent and Miss Carlson began handing out the test sheets. "How are you feeling, Jason?" Miss

Carlson asked as she came to his and Rachel's table.

"I'm better than I was, thank you, miss," Jason replied.

"Good to hear that," his teacher said, and gave them their test sheets.

They finished the test at half past eleven and everyone went off to lunch. Jason was walking down to the lunch hall, he wanted to call Kate and see how the investigation was going and if there was anything he could do to help. "Hey Jason, wait up!" Rachel was running down the corridor, trying to catch up with him.

"Where are you sitting for lunch?" she asked him as they carried on walking down the corridor.

"Probably in the lunch hall as usual," he told her.

Suddenly Jason stopped. He heard something. Someone was coming up the stairs from the main doors. He heard footsteps, footsteps that sounded familiar, the same kind of shoes worn by the zombies that attacked him and Kate at the museum, and they were heading his way. "Excuse me, what are you doing here?" he heard a teacher ask one of them, but the footsteps were getting closer. "Excuse me!" the teacher repeated. The zombies came from behind the corner and spotted Jason immediately and reached for their guns.

"Get down!" Jason shouted and pulled Rachel to the ground. The next thing anyone knew, the zombies were firing at anyone that moved. Luckily no one got hurt – everyone in the corridor moved out of the way the moment they saw the guns. "What the hell do they want?" Rachel asked Jason as they crawled behind a cabinet towards one of the classrooms.

Jason and Rachel ran into the classroom and shut the door behind them. "Help me block the door," Jason said to Rachel.

"What's going on out there?" the teacher in the classroom asked them both. They had walked in on a class.

"Some people have showed up shooting everyone!" Rachel told the teacher as another series of shots were fired.

"Oh my god!" one of the students in the class screamed.

"Calm down everyone," the teacher said to the class.

"We need to call the police," another student said.

"I'll do it," Jason said as he got his phone out and ran into the teacher's office while the teacher helped Rachel push his desk in front of the door. Jason stepped into the English teacher's office; he didn't understand how those two zombies had got into the school. Dwight had assigned two Hunters to watch the school in case this sort of thing happened, what the hell had happened to them? Jason dialled in Kate's number and called her. "C'mon, pick up!" he said as the phone kept ringing.

"Hello," Kate said as she answered the phone.

"Kate, it's me, there are zombies here at the school!" he told her.

"Is that gunfire I can hear?" Kate asked him.

"Yes, they've got guns and I think they're after me," Jason explained.

"I'm on my way," Kate said, and the last thing Jason heard before he ended the call was Kate running down a hall shouting for Dwight.

"Dwight, Jason just called. Harfang's zombies are at the school!" Kate said as she ran into his office. Mark was there with a test result file.

"When I was at school I used to think there were zombies there, turned out it was the boys of the school's football team," Mark said.

Dwight stifled a laugh. "Alright," he said, getting serious. "Mark, there may be casualties there. I want you to get a medical team together and go down there with Kate and the squat team." Dwight put down his drink and got up. "I'll get in touch with the two Hunters I placed outside the school. They'd better not be on their lunch break," he told them, and left his office.

"Come on," Kate said to Mark, and they left the office hastily.

Jason came off the phone. "Police are on their way," he told everyone as he came out of the office.

Suddenly someone shot at the classroom door.

"Oh my god!" one of the other students screamed.

"Help me open these windows someone!" the teacher said as he ran over to the windows. One of the boys came and helped him.

"We can't get out that way, we're on the second floor!" one of the girls said. As she looked down through the window another around of shots were fired through the door.

"What do they want?" another student asked, scared.

"I don't know," Jason lied. He knew exactly what they wanted... him.

Kate's car pulled up outside the school; students and teachers were running out of the building. The A.R.V. van pulled up beside her car. Kate spotted the car from which the Hunters were watching the school; she walked over to it and looked inside. Both men were dead. "Judging by the contact burns on the sides of their heads, I'd say they were shot up close and they probably used a silencer which could explain why no one heard," Mark told her as he examined the bodies.

"They're not using silencers now," Kate said, and went to talk to the Firearms Unit team. "Alright fellas, we've got civilians trapped in there as well as Jason and I refuse to let anything happen to him." She pulled out her gun and they all followed her into the school. They came up the first corridor and saw three students and a teacher hurt badly. "Mark, get these people out of here and get them taken care of," Kate told Mark.

"On it," he said as his medical team went to help the civilians wounded. Kate and the team carried on down the corridor and turned to where the zombies were trying to break into a classroom. "Freeze!" Kate yelled and pointed her gun at them. The zombies turned and fired at her.

Jason heard Kate yell at the zombies – she had come with help; there was hope for them yet. But suddenly he heard gunfire, then someone's body dropped. They'd killed her. Jason felt like he had just lost a sister, even though he had only known her a few days. She had been kind to him and made his werewolfism feel like it was natural. "Is anyone hurt in there?" a voice asked. Jason felt a sudden joy inside him. It was Kate who had spoken.

"We're fine," the teacher replied. Jason, Rachel and another student began removing the desk from the door. Kate came into the classroom.

"We have the two who attacked you, we had no choice but to shoot them in defence," Kate explained to the class.

"Who were they?" the teacher asked her.

"Part of a terrorist group," Kate lied.

The bodies of the two zombies were being loaded into an HQ van when Dorian arrived on the scene. Kate was busy finishing giving orders to some officers when Dorian walked up to her. "Is Jason alright?" he asked Kate as the officers walked away.

"He's fine, we got there just in time," Kate told him as they walked to his car.

"It might be best to put Jason in protective custody until this case is closed," Dorian said as he opened the driver's side door of his car.

"Harfang has eyes and ears everywhere. He knew which school Jason goes too, he knew which hospital he was sent to when he was bitten and that he and I had gone to the Natural History Museum. If we put him in protective custody, Harfang will find out where Jason is soon enough," she explained.

"What do you recommend we do then?" Dorian asked her. "We'll send someone to stay at Jason's house to guard him," Kate said.

"Good idea," Dorian replied. "So I think it might

be best if you stay with him."

"What!" Kate gasped.

"It was your idea and his mother already knows you," Dorian explained, then got in the car. "By the way, the Chalice will be arriving at Heathrow airport tonight at eight. You and Jason should be there to make sure it's delivered to HQ."

"Are you sure it will be safer there then at the museum?" Kate asked him.

"More than safe, despite the attack in the parking lot yesterday, no one has ever broken into the Underground," he said, and shut the car door then drove off.

Chapter 20

Special Delivery

Jason's mum was nearly in tears when Jason came home. "I heard what happened at the school," she said, and hugged Jason the moment he stepped through the door.

"Mrs Wilson," Kate said as she stepped inside the house, "I've been assigned to stay with your family in case any more of these men try to harm you in any way," she explained.

"Thank you Detective Joans," Mrs Wilson said as she let Kate in. "That's extremely kind of Scotland Yard."

"I'll show you to the guest room," Jason said and led Kate upstairs.

The guest room had a bed in the corner, a bedside table stood next to it with a lamp on top, and a chest of drawers stood on the other side of the room. The window had dark emerald curtains and the wallpaper was a pale green with a wood panel floor, and the sheets on the bed were a lush leaf-colour green with a set of yellow towels on the bed. "You must have a lot of people over," Kate said as she examined the room.

"Mostly people from where Dad works coming over to spend the night before going to board meetings the next day," Jason explained, "but he's over in America meeting one of the American branches of the company."

"The Chalice will be arriving at Heathrow airport at eight o' clock tonight," Kate told Jason as she unpacked her bag. "We'll be leave here at six to go back to HQ first for a briefing on what we're actually going to do at the airport," she explained.

"Well I'll tell my mum we have to go back to Scotland Yard to help fill in reports on what happened at school today," Jason said and went downstairs.

At six o' clock, Jason and Kate left his house. Jason kissed his mum goodbye and said not to wait up for them if they were late back. They drove into London and parked in the abandoned parking lot as usual and entered the elevator. "Do you think it'll get nasty at the airport if Harfang is there?" Jason asked as they descended in the elevator. "Most likely," Kate replied, "which is why we're going prepared."

The doors opened and in the main hall were probably two to three dozen men and women in black wearing Kevlar bulletproof vests and all of them armed with guns. "This is what you call prepared!" Jason said as they stepped out of the elevator.

"Sort of," Kate said, and they walked off towards Dwight's office. Dorian and Mark were sat with Dwight, waiting for Jason and Kate. "I hope we're not late," Kate said to them as she entered the office.

"You're a few seconds late but I'll forgive you,"

Dwight joked. "Alright," he said as he got up, "you all know how important this is. If Harfang gets his hands on the Chalice, all hell will break loose and we'll have a vampire uprising on our hands and I don't need to tell you how dangerous that possibility could be," Dwight explained. "We're expected at Heathrow. I asked the Prime Minister to clear it for us and we have permission to take the Chalice back here to the Underground so we have an advantage on Harfang, which is we can get in and out of Heathrow and avoid any trouble."

"You'll need this," Dorian said to Jason and handed him a box. Inside was a crossbow the size of a revolver and a pack of arrows. "There's a chance we might run into trouble if Harfang shows up and you're not trained to use a gun or old enough for that matter," Dorian told Jason.

"But a crossbow is fine for someone my age?" Jason replied.

"Well just don't tell anyone," Dorian responded.

There were six vehicles in total, Dorian's car, an armoured car which would be used to take the Chalice back to the Underground, and four A.R.V vans. Kate, Jason, and Mark drove in the armoured car while Dwight and Dorian led the way in Dorian's car. "What's going to happen again?" Jason asked, making sure he understood the plan.

"We arrive at the airport," Mark explained, "and then we load the Chalice into the car and drive off before Harfang and his zombie men arrive."

"Is it really going to be that easy?" Jason asked them both.

"I hope so," Kate replied.

They soon arrived at Heathrow airport and were parked in the landing bay. The plane had arrived a few minutes before they had and there were people outside already waiting for them. Dwight got out of the car and handed the men some forms; they read the forms then nodded to the people on the plane unloading baggage and they unloaded a small black crate. Dorian got out and walked over to the crate once it was lowered down onto a conveyer belt and opened it up – the Chalice was inside. Dorian turned to Kate and nodded, it was the real one. "Come on," Kate said to Jason and Mark. They got out and approached the crate; Dorian had already shut the lid. The crate, luckily enough, had a handle. Mark picked it up and carried it back to the car.

"How much does this thing weigh?" Mark asked Dorian as he carried back to the car.

"It's made of thirty pieces of silver," Dorian explained, "and the inside of box is lined with lead."

Kate went to the back of the armoured car and opened the boot, suddenly there came the screech of car tyres. Jason turned around fast and saw a black car and two black vans speeding towards them. They stopped and zombies came running out with machine guns.

"Shit, get down!" Dorian shouted, and the gunfire came.

Chapter 21

Gunned In

No sooner had everyone dropped to the ground, the zombies fired their machine guns. The air smelt of gunpowder and the only sound that could be heard was the sound of death coming from the machine guns. Dwight pulled out his radio from his pocket. "Where the bloody hell is backup?" he asked on the radio.

Suddenly the A.R.V van doors opened and armed troops stormed out and fired back at the zombies. "I see Harfang!" Kate told Dorian.

"Looks like we're going to have to fight our way out," Mark said and got out his gun. He kept the crate close to him. Jason got out the crossbow Dorian had given him and loaded an arrow into it.

"Kate, you, Jason, and Mark get that crate out of here and make sure none of Harfang's men get their hands on it!" Dwight said to Kate.

"On it," she replied, then took out her gun and made her way to Mark and the Chalice.

Jason managed to crawl his way over to Mark. "You alright?" Mark asked Jason, who was now a nervous and nearly sweating.

"I'm not used to being shot at," he told Mark.

"Neither am I; I'm just the pathologist who also works in the forensics lab," Mark replied.

Dorian ran and knelt behind a set of stairs used to let people on and off planes when his phone rang, it was Harfang. "Harfang, you don't have to do this," Dorian said.

"Then give me what I want!" Harfang replied.

"You have no right to take it!" Dorian told him. The gunfire sounded nearer.

"I have every right! That Chalice belongs to all vampires."

"And all vampires try to forget it does!" Dorian replied. "The silver used to make the Chalice was seen as sin against God, the silver that had a role in Judas's betrayal of Jesus that cursed him and turned him into the first vampire. People who were bitten and turned into vampires have worked hard to break away from the addictions for blood and carry on with their lives. All you want to do is use the Chalice to turn them into savage monsters under your control."

"They're ungrateful!" Harfang shouted down the phone. "They've been given the gift of immortality and all they want is to live as filthy mortal humans! But when I use the Chalice, not only will I have control over the vampires that still walk among us but also those who were killed for sharing my beliefs."

"They were murderers and terrorists!" Dorian said.

"Because they did not share your beliefs you call them criminals." Harfang laughed. "They knew the truth, Gray. They knew that the Underground only exists to keep people believing the world is normal; you try to make the world match the people's vision of what a normal world should be, well they've had their turn, it's our turn now."

"Do you seriously expect me to believe you want to make a better world? All you'll do with the Chalice is use it to kill all humans on the planet and lock them up like animals."

There was silence, Harfang hadn't replied to what Dorian had just said. Finally the silence was broken when Harfang spoke again. "Then we have nothing else to say to one another," Harfang said.

"One more thing, Harfang," Dorian replied, then spun round and stabbed Harfang in the shoulder. The blade became stuck in one of the steps on the stairs.

"Ah! You bastard, Gray!" Harfang spat. Dorian looked at him.

"If you're going to shoot me, don't do it when my back's turned." A gun dropped out of Harfang's hand – he had been planning to sneak up on Dorian and shoot him from behind, although it wouldn't have killed Dorian, it might have be enough to knock him out for thirty minutes or so. "Good luck trying to pull that out," Dorian said. "The entire sword is made of silver and coated in holy water for good measures."

Dorian picked the gun up off the floor and left Harfang stuck with the sword in his shoulder.

Kate made her way back to the armoured car and knelt down next to Mark. "Dwight's ordered us to get the Chalice out of here by any means necessary," she told them.

"Have you any idea how we're going to get it out?" Jason asked her.

"There's a plane across from here getting ready for take-off," Mark said. "If we can get past these guys we could hide the Chalice on the cargo section of the plane and have it taken to another country, and it's out of Harfang's reach for now."

"Better idea," Kate said. "See that over there?" She pointed to a gallon tank of gasoline. "Harfang's zombies take a special kind of medication that prevents the decomposition of the user's body," she explained.

"I see what you're getting at," Mark replied, smiling.

"What?" Jason asked, confused.

"The medication they take doesn't prevent them from burning," Kate told Jason, "and heat increases the rate of decay on a body."

Jason grinned at Kate, he knew what she was planning. "Does anyone have a light on them?" Jason asked them both.

"Dwight does," Kate replied.

Dwight was knelt next to one of his men; they both had a gun in their hand. "Dwight!" Mark shouted from over from the armoured car.

"What?" Dwight asked as he looked over at the three of them.

"We need your match box!" Kate told him. "We're going to set a fire around the zombies," she explained.

"Brilliant idea!" Dwight replied.

"We're going to need some help with the gasoline," Mark added, and Dwight nodded then turned to the man knelt next to him.

"Get over there and help them," he ordered the armed officer.

"Yes sir!" the officer replied.

"Take these with you." Dwight handed the officer his box of matches then carried on shooting at the zombies. While Mark and the armed officer were busy with the gasoline tank, Jason and Kate loaded the Chalice into the armoured car.

"Jason," Kate said as he loaded the box into the car, "as soon as the match is lit we're getting out of here as fast as we can and there's a chance this plan with the gasoline may not work, so whatever happens, keep your head down and try not to get hurt."

The gasoline had leaked out towards the zombies, close enough to catch them but not close enough for them to notice it. The armed officer got in the car with Kate and Jason, leaving Mark to light the match. The moment Mark lit the match he dropped it onto the gasoline trail and got into the car. The fire spread rapidly around the zombies; they didn't even know what hit them until they were trapped. Dwight had ordered the other troops to do the same thing and soon the circle of fire rose and became even hotter. "Keep firing!" Dwight ordered, and all that could be heard when the armoured car left the airport was gunfire and the crackling of the flames.

"We're going to have a hard time explaining this to the police," Mark said as he looked out the passenger side window. People were watching the fire and on their phones, no doubt calling their friends and the police.

When they arrived back at HQ, they were greeted by security who escorted them back inside. Security had been tightened since the attack in the car park and more security had been posted both in the car park and in the Underground. "We'll take this to the examination room," Kate told the armed officer, who nodded and went off down one of the corridors.

"What's the examination room?" Jason asked her as they walked past the Hall of Records.

"The artefact examination room is where the artefacts we get such as the Chalice are examined and catalogued, and then the artefact is taken down to the Vault, which is where we stored all the other artefacts we've found," Kate explained.

"Right, I'm going back down to the lab," Mark told them, and headed down the stairs. They arrived at the examination room and Kate handed the crate to a woman who worked there.

"Call me when it's done," Kate said to the woman, then left the examination room.

Chapter 22

The Vault

Dwight and Dorian had stayed behind at the airport to explain to the police that they had been at the airport to prevent a terrorist attack, which the police had believed after a very detailed explanation and a call from Downing Street. "We're going to have to stop saying it's a terrorist attack soon," Dwight told Dorian as they got into Dorian's car.

"I suppose we could go back to saying it was Nazi spies," Dorian suggested as they left Heathrow.

"The Underground stopped using that excuse before I even started," Dwight said.

They had been driving for nearly two hours when Dorian spoke again. "I can't believe Harfang got away again," he told Dwight.

"We'll get him soon enough," Dwight assured them as they passed a field. "We have the Chalice, he's bound to try and steal it."

Kate woke up at five past eight. After she had a shower and got dressed she went downstairs, where Mrs Wilson was making breakfast. "Morning Detective Joans," she said as Kate walked into the kitchen.

"Good morning Mrs Wilson," Kate replied and poured herself some coffee.

"Please, call me Helen," Mrs Wilson said, and placed some bacon onto three plates. Jason came downstairs and sat down at the table. "Slept well?" his mum asked him, and placed a plate on the table.

"Fine thanks," he replied.

"I take it school is still closed," Jason said as his mum and Kate sat down at the table.

"I'm afraid so," Mrs Wilson told him, "after those men attacked the school, parents aren't letting their children go back there until there is new security installed for their children's safety," she explained.

"Looks like another day at work with me then," Kate said to Jason.

As soon as they had breakfast they left for the Underground. "I take it we'll be trying to catch Harfang now that the Chalice is locked away in the examination room," Jason said as they drove down the road.

"Undoubtedly," Kate replied.

They arrived at HQ a little after eleven; Mark was sat in the Hall of Records reading while he had his morning coffee. "Morning," Kate said to him as they sat down at his table.

"Hmmm," Mark replied, still reading his book.

"Is he usually like this in the morning?" Jason asked Kate.

"Yes," Mark said, not listening to what they were saying.

"He's always doing this in the morning when he arrives," Kate explained. "Watch... Mark, Jason turned into a werewolf again last night and killed everyone in his neighbourhood," she lied.

"Good, good," Mark muttered, and took a sip of coffee.

"Oh for God's sake, Mark!"

Mark jumped when Kate shouted his name.

"What?" he asked her, startled.

"Have you heard a single word we've said?" she asked him.

"Maybe, I don't know, I was busy reading," Mark replied.

"Unbelievable," Kate said. Just then her phone rang and she answered it. "Hello, right, ok we're on our way." Kate came off the phone and turned to Jason. "They're done with the Chalice," she told him, "we're going to pick it up now."

"Fine by me," Jason said, and followed Kate out of the Hall of Records. "Where do we need to take it now?" Jason asked Kate as they walked down the corridor.

"The Vault," Kate replied. "It's where we store all artefacts that are deemed too dangerous for the public. It's beneath the Hall of Records, the lowest part of London; it runs directly beneath the sewers and there's only one way in and out of there."

They arrived at the examination room, where the woman was waiting for them. "It's all yours now, detective. We've catalogued it and examined every inch of it. It's the real Chalice, making this a category

X artefact," the woman explained to them both.

"Into the Vaults it goes then," Kate said, and picked up the box, and Jason followed her out of the room.

There was only one way in and out of the Vault – a trap door in the Hall of Records that led to a spiral staircase that took you to the Vault beneath the sewers of London, and the only way to get access to the staircase was through the Librarians, who worked in the Hall of Records. There were assistant librarians who worked in the Hall of Records, but there were only ever two Librarians – these were men and women who studied and stored all artefacts that were either too dangerous for the public or unknown to the public. The Librarians who worked at the HQ in London were two old men – a tall man with white hair who wore glasses, and a short man with dark grey hair. Kate and Jason arrived at their reception desk which was located on the top floor of the Hall of Records, which overlooked the entire library.

Kate knocked on the door and inside, someone could be heard dropping what seemed to sound like a stack of books. "Oh now look what you've done!" a man shouted. Kate knocked a second time. "Coming, coming," said the man, and a short man opened the door. "Detective Joans, to what do I owe this pleasure?" the short man asked.

"We've brought you something," Kate said, and held up the box.

"I see," the man said, and stood aside and Kate walked in, followed by Jason. The office was full of old fashioned filing cabinets and files stacked everywhere, along with some dusty old leather-bound books with the leather peeling off; two desks stood facing one another in the middle of the office and in the corner was a work bench with tools and equipment needed to repair and preserve old books.

The tall man was bent down, picking up some files and one or two books. He looked up and saw Kate and Jason. "Oh good, company," he said, and placed the files he'd picked up on his desk then straightened his shirt. "How are you, detective?" he asked Kate, and hugged her.

"I'm fine thanks Douglas," Kate said.

Douglas turned and looked at Jason. "Ah, you must be Jason," Douglas said, and held out his hand for Jason to shake. "I've seen you in the Hall once or twice this week."

"Honestly, do I have to do everything around here!" the short man said, and went over to pick up the rest of the files. "Allow me to introduce my colleague, Mr Oswald Gates."

Oswald looked up at Douglas. "Why is it, I always have to finish cleaning up for you?" Oswald said, and slammed the rest of the files onto Douglas's desk. "Every time we have a visitor over, you forget what you're doing and go to talk to them. You'd have made a rubbish detective." Oswald was wearing a tan brown suit and a pair of latex gloves. Judging by the fact the lamp on the workbench was switched on, Jason guessed Oswald had been in the middle of restoring an old book when Kate had knocked on the door.

"We've brought a category X artefact for the Vault," Kate explained to them both.

"What's category X mean?" Jason asked.

"It means extremely dangerous," Douglas replied before Oswald could answer the question.

"I was about to tell him that!" Oswald said, annoyed.

"Then why didn't you say it first, hmm?" Douglas asked.

"Look, before you two enter another argument, can you please take this down to the Vault?" Kate interrupted.

"Fine," Oswald said, and Kate handed him the box.

"I don't suppose you've seen the Vault yet, have you?" Douglas said to Jason.

"He's not been properly evaluated yet," Oswald reminded Douglas. "He's still classed as a civilian and civilians aren't allowed access to the Vault."

"Civilians aren't supposed to know the Underground exists and that vampires and werewolves exist as well, but he already does," Douglas pointed out.

Oswald frowned then looked at Jason. "Alright, but if we get into trouble for this it's entirely your fault," Oswald said to Douglas, then left the office.

"C'mon," Kate said to Jason, and they followed Oswald and Douglas out of their office.

They went back down to the lower level of the Hall of Records and passed a few rows of reading desks. They stepped through an archway that led to another section of the library – no one was in this part of the Hall of Records. Oswald handed the box back to Kate and he and Douglas walked over to the side of a long, tall bookcase. A small keyhole was in the bookcase which could be passed undetected to anyone if they wanted to try and break into the Vault. Douglas took out a key from around his neck and put it in the keyhole and turned it. A small panel popped open next to the keyhole and inside was another keyhole and a pull-out lever next to it. Oswald took out his key and placed it in the keyhole and turned, then he took hold of the lever and pulled it out of the bookcase and the tiles on the floor began to rise and open up to reveal a spiral staircase made of stone.

"After you," Douglas said to Oswald, who had already taken the box back off of Kate and began descending the stairs. Kate followed Oswald, then Jason went down after Kate, then finally Douglas went down last, and once they were down out of sight, the trap door closed up.

It was getting darker as they went deeper down the stairs. Jason only then realised none of them had a flashlight on them or even a match. Suddenly the staircase brightened and Jason could see an iron door up ahead. "Where is it?" Jason heard Oswald mutter to himself.

"You haven't lost it again, have you?" Douglas asked Oswald from the back of the line.

"Of course I haven't lost it!" Oswald replied.

"That means you've lost it," Douglas said and looked at Kate. "You know he lost it last year, he had me look all around the Hall for it, only to discover it was in his bedside table at home. He even got his wife to drive down here to give it him and she's not supposed to know the Vault exists."

"I never told her the Vault existed, all I said was it was my spare credit card, trouble was though, that woman knows what all my credit cards look like anyway," Oswald explained as he searched his pockets, "so when she asked me what it really was, I told her it was a new account I took out that she didn't know about and that I was booking us a holiday on a cruise liner for a month for our anniversary."

"And so he had to really book a month holiday on a cruise!" Douglas laughed. "You should have seen his face when he saw how much it would cost him!"

Jason and Kate couldn't help laughing.

"Found it," Oswald said at last, "it was in my wallet the whole time."

"That's probably because your wife thinks it's a credit card," Kate said, amused. Oswald didn't say anything, he turned to the electric lock and slid the key card through the lock. It beeped and the door unlocked. As soon as everyone was inside, Oswald shut the door and it automatically locked.

"Welcome to the Vault," Douglas said to Jason. Jason stood in amazement, the room they were in was round, with bookcases covering every wall. Beyond that room was what Jason could only describe as a museum, full of antiques and ancient artefacts. The circular room seemed more like a study, with a table in the centre and four chairs surrounding it, with a reading lamp in the middle of the table. They stepped through the arch, passed through the study and into the museum section of the Vault. Jason kept looking at his surroundings; all the artefacts were stored in either glass cabinets or on shelves. Jason could have spent hours in here looking at all these artefacts and learning about them, but suddenly remembered they were locked away down here for a reason, because they were too dangerous.

Oswald and Douglas led them to a fence that had a sign warning people the fence had electricity running through it; there was another electric lock which was connected to the fence door. This time Douglas took out a key card and slid it down the lock, and the door opened. On the other side of the fence were more glass cabinets, but these had security sensors attached to them. "This is where we store all category X artefacts," Oswald explained as he opened up the box. "This area alone has the highest level of security in the entire Underground." Oswald turned to Douglas, who was putting on a pair of latex gloves. "Is the cabinet set?" he asked Douglas.

"One moment," Douglas said, and typed in a code. The red light on an empty cabinet flashed green. Oswald gently took the Chalice out of its box and carefully placed it inside the cabinet, then shut the cabinet door. The sensor light turned red again and Douglas wrote on a plaque on the top of the cabinet: *Judas Chalice*. "Well that's that," Douglas said as they began to head out of the Vault.

"That's it?" Jason said, somewhat disappointed. "Shouldn't you have people on guard down here or something?"

"Whatever for?" Oswald asked him. "We've got state of the art security systems installed down here and locks that require a special key to unlock them, and if anyone manages to acquire a copy of the keys, they won't work because the locks are designed to know the difference between a copy and the real keys."

"And then there's the key cards," Douglas said as they passed through the study. "If anyone tries to use a copy of the key cards on the locks then the locks shut down and the entire Vault goes under lockdown, which sends an alarm throughout every computer in HQ."

They stopped in the study and Oswald walked over to a book that sat on a stand that stood next to the door. He opened the book on a blank page and wrote down the date, then wrote down the time when the Chalice was brought to the vault, then he and Douglas signed the log; after that was done they all left the study, locked up, and went back up into the Hall of Records.

Chapter 23

On the Run

"Kate!" Dorian was running into the Hall of Records; he was wearing the same clothes he'd worn yesterday. "I just got a call; apparently Harfang has left his hideout in the church. We're going over there now."

Kate turned to Jason.

"Jason, I want you to stay here," Kate told Jason.

"Why?" Jason asked.

"After what happened last night, I want you to stay here and practice firing the crossbow Dorian gave you," Kate explained.

"Fine," Jason said, and went off to the training room downstairs.

"I still think we should have brought backup," Kate said to Dorian as they drove down the streets of London.

"We don't need backup," Dorian replied.

"We're about to go into a criminal vampire's crypt, I'm pretty sure we need backup."

"An empty criminal vampire crypt," Dorian corrected. "Besides, he won't be coming back, he knows that we know he's hiding at the church."

"And we know, that he knows, that we know where he's hiding," Kate added.

They arrived at St. Andros church; the doors were open and the windows were still boarded up. Dorian and Kate got out of the car and approached the front doors. Kate got out her gun and Dorian pulled out his sword. On the count of three they entered the church, Kate with her gun pointing in front and Dorian holding his sword in his left hand and his walking stick in his right. "Clear," Dorian said to Kate once they knew the main hall was clear.

Kate opened a side door and checked the cupboard – it was empty except for a few cobwebs. "Clear," she said, then they walked up the stairs and came to the door of the room Dorian had crept into the last time he and Kate were here. Kate grabbed hold of the door handle and counted to three again, then swung the door open. It was empty. All the crates containing Harfang's own artefacts were gone; the freezer unit was gone as well, but the room wasn't entirely empty – a body lay on the floor.

"We'd better call this in," Dorian said, and got out his phone to call HQ. The body was male and his throat looked as though it had been ripped out.

* * *

Harfang walked up to the house. He was wearing a pinstriped suit and was carrying a briefcase. He rang the doorbell and waited patiently – patience was something Harfang could be good at when he was in the right mood and he hadn't had much patience since Crown was arrested, and had even less since they lost the Chalice. Mrs Wilson opened the door and Harfang smiled.

"Excuse me," he said kindly, "is this Wilkins Street?" he asked Mrs Wilson.

"I'm afraid not, sorry," Mrs Wilson replied.

"I'm sorry for wasting your time," Harfang said, "but could you tell me how to get there?" he asked her.

"Yes, you turn down the street, keep going, then turn left and you should be there," she explained.

"Thank you," Harfang said, then he groaned.

"Are you alright?" Mrs Wilson asked Harfang.

"No," Harfang said to her. "I was in an accident a while back and I got stabbed in the shoulder. I'm in the military you see, and I've just got back. May I use your bathroom to replace the bandage on it?" he lied.

"Of course, but you really should go to a doctor about it. I suppose that's why you're going to Wilkins Street," Mrs Wilson said as she let Harfang in.

"Yes, but I should have changed the bandaged before I left my flat," Harfang went on as he walked up the stairs.

"The bathroom is the first door on the right, there should be some bandages in the cabinet," she told him. Harfang stepped into the bathroom and opened his briefcase. He removed a small green medicine bottle and silently opened the bathroom door and stepped out onto the landing without being heard, something vampires were good at. Harfang found

Jason's room without any difficulty; he walked over to Jason's bedside table and opened one of the drawers. Jason's tablets were just sitting there, making it easy for Harfang to switch the bottles. Harfang shut the bathroom door and went back downstairs. He pulled a small umbrella out of his briefcase. "Thank you for letting me use your facilities," Harfang said to Mrs Wilson.

"I hope your shoulder feels better, you really don't need that though, the sun's out," Mrs Wilson nodded to the window.

"I have a skin condition," Harfang said which was technically true. "I developed it after spending a year out in the desert," he lied.

"I'm sorry to hear that," Mrs Wilson said to Harfang. "I hope your doctor's appointment goes well."

"Thank you," Harfang replied and left the house; his umbrella sheltered him from the sun until he arrived at his van and climbed into the back and hid in the darkness of his coffin while his driver drove him away.

Chapter 24

The Scent of Vampire

Jason was in the training room, practicing firing the crossbow. It turned out that it was a lot more difficult than it looked. Jason loaded the crossbow again and aimed it at the target board, focused and fired. He missed the centre of the man on the board but managed to hit the target in the shoulder. "Not bad," Jason said, then loaded the crossbow again and this time he hit the target in the crotch.

"Impressive," Dwight said. He had been watching Jason practice the whole time. "You're doing fine for someone who's never fired a crossbow before," Dwight remarked as he took another crossbow off a rack.

"Thank you," Jason replied and loaded his crossbow again. "Oswald said something about me not being properly evaluated yet, what did he mean?" Jason asked as Dwight loaded his own crossbow.

"He meant your evaluation into working for the Underground," Dwight explained. "We test our interns to see if they're fit to become Hunters for the Underground or if they're more suited to a desk job." Dwight fired his crossbow and hit his target in the centre.

"You're good at this," Jason admitted.

"Thank you," Dwight said. "Of course after this case, you'll be allowed to decide whether or not you want to work here, either way we'll still get you the medication that you require."

All of a sudden, Dwight's phone started ringing. Dwight answered it. "Dwight. What? A murder! And Harfang's left nothing to hint where he's going? Right, ok then, I'll send Mark down with a forensics team to search for any evidence that may be useful to us." Dwight put his phone down. "That was Dorian," he told Jason. "They've found a body at the church, possibly killed by Harfang."

"At least we know he's not at the church," Jason said, "which means he could be getting ready to break in here and steal the Chalice."

"That's impossible," Dwight remarked. "Security's at its highest, the Librarians are the only two people who have keys into the Vault and there are only two ways into HQ – through the parking lot and through Parliament." Dwight contacted Mark and told him to make his way down to St. Andros church with a forensics team.

Jason was sent with them to see if he could pick up Harfang's scent, something werewolves are extremely good at during the day or night.

They arrived at St. Andros and the forensics team were the first ones in, a couple of officers from HQ had gone with them to the church and kept guard outside. Jason stepped into the church and all of a sudden he picked up the most bizarre smell. He couldn't describe it and he couldn't quite place where he had smelt it before. "Jason," Dorian called from upstairs and came down to him. "How's the training going?" he asked Jason.

"Fine," Jason said. He was too distracted by that smell to listen to Dorian.

"You've picked up a scent, haven't you?" Dorian said, and Jason turned to look at him.

"I think so, it's hard to say," Jason admitted, and suddenly he was hit by another smell and went off down to the vicar's old office. The door was old and weathered and it creaked when Jason opened the door; inside, the wallpaper's colour had faded and was peeling off the walls. The office was empty.

"The scent's really strong in here," Jason told Dorian as they circled the room. Dorian spotted soil on the wooden floor.

"This must be where they kept Harfang's earth box," he said to Jason, and knelt down to examine the soil. "This might be able to tell us where Harfang's been hiding the past few years," Dorian explained, then waved a forensic scientist into the room. "Take samples of this soil and take it back to the labs for testing and find out where it came from," Dorian told the forensic assistant.

Mark examined the body, checking to see if the victim gave much of a struggle when he was killed, and tried to estimate the time of death. "It doesn't seem your victim gave up much of struggle," he told Kate, and he examined the damage on the victim's throat. "This is definitely the handiwork of a vampire," he continued, then he examined the victim's arm. He saw a small puncture marks, indicating this man had used a syringe, but for what? Drugs maybe? Or something that might have been important to this man, something that might explain why time of death was hard to establish with the victim.

"Judging by these puncture wounds on the victim's arm I believe he might be a zombie, explaining why it's impossible to establish a time of death," Mark explained.

"Why would Harfang kill one of his own zombies?" Kate said.

Mark looked up at her. "Maybe he did something wrong or was going to turn himself in to the Underground and so Harfang had him killed to silence him," Mark suggested. Mark motioned for his two assistants to place the body on a stretcher and take it back to HQ. Jason passed the assistants on their way out of the room. Kate looked at him in surprise as he walked around the room.

"What's wrong?" Kate asked Jason and he stopped.

"Harfang was in here," Jason said, "his scent's quite strong up here too. He must have spent a lot of time upstairs," Jason told Kate.

Dorian joined them in the room.

"There's another scent," Jason said, a little confused. "This one matches the smell in the main hall."

"That'll be a zombie," Dorian explained.

"I'm going to go back to HQ with the body and see what else I can find that might help us," Mark told them and walked out of the room and made his way downstairs to the van.

"We might as well go too," Dorian said, "there's nothing left here that could help find Harfang."

Kate nodded in agreement and Jason followed them out of the room.

Chapter 25

The Werewolf Loose

in the Underground

Dorian, Kate, and Jason went back to Jason's house first so Jason could take his tablets. They pulled up outside his house and Jason got out of the car. Dorian and Kate waited for him in the car as he went inside.

"Mum," Jason called out as he walked in through the front door.

"I'm in the kitchen," his mum answered back. "Your sister just called to say she's coming back on Friday," she told Jason.

"Brilliant!" Jason said. He hardly ever saw his sister since she'd gone back to college.

"And your dad said he's sorry but he can't get back early, turns out the people he's gone to see want to sign the deal with the company after all."

Jason nodded then went upstairs and went into his room and got out his tablets. He didn't know how long he could hide what he was actually doing from them; he didn't like lying to his family but he was afraid what they might think if he told them he was a werewolf and was working with a special kind of police that investigated crimes involving vampires, werewolves, zombies, and a great deal of other things that were thought to be fictional. Would they believe him? And if so would they be scared of him, hate him, or love him just the same?

He took his tablets, then went back downstairs. "I'm going to be back late tonight," he told his mother as he walked into the kitchen. "Kate's got to show me how to store evidence once a case is closed," he lied.

"That's fine," his mother replied. "I'm glad you're enjoying your work experience," she said to Jason. "With any luck one day you'll want to join the police force."

"That's still open for debate," Jason told her, then kissed her on the cheek and left.

Jason got back in the car with Kate and Dorian. As soon as he put his seatbelt on they left for HQ. As they pulled into the car park, Dorian spotted someone out next to the elevator doors; it was the red-haired secretary from the front desk in the entrance hall of the Underground. He spotted Dorian and Kate the moment they parked, when Jason got out of the car he walked away.

"What's wrong with him?" Kate said as the secretary stepped into the elevator.

"Probably scared of Jason," Dorian told them as they walked towards the elevator. "You'd be surprised how many people here are scared of werewolves."

This didn't make Jason feel any better but he didn't say anything.

They took the elevator back down into HQ and passed the secretary, who was now hurrying back to his desk in the entrance room. "He looks nervous," Jason remarked as the secretary went down a corridor. Mark was in the morgue, finishing his autopsy on the victim from the church when Dorian, Kate, and Jason arrived. He looked up at them and took off his gloves, and went to wash his hands in a sink.

"He was definitely a zombie," Mark informed them as he washed his hands.

"How do you know that?" Jason asked.

Mark dried his hands then picked up a vial from a rack next to the slab with the body on, a brown liquid was inside it. "His blood was full of this stuff," Mark explained. "It's the medication zombies use to stay alive. Once you've become a zombie, you have twenty-four hours to take this stuff or you begin to decompose and your mind will make you a savage like in all those zombie movies, but you'll be happy to know I've figured out why Harfang killed him."

"Why?" Dorian asked.

"I just finished reading the reports from the workers at the tip in Sheffield who told us how they found the body of Marry Creed. Apparently a man matching this zombie's description was seen before the tip closed the night before her body was found. This man was the last person at the tip to drop rubbish off, according to the witness' report, he dropped off three black bags full with junk and a tatty rolled up rug. Anyone care to guess what was in the rug?" Mark asked.

"Marry Creed's body," Kate said.

"So Harfang killed this zombie because he left her body somewhere where she'd be found easily," Jason said.

"And as soon as Harfang discovered we were looking into her death, he knew we'd soon discover what he was after, so he tied up loose ends by killing this zombie," Dorian finished off.

"So now we're back to square one," Kate said. "We don't know where Harfang is, all we know is he wants the chalice and we don't know how he plans to take it from us."

"Maybe he plans to dig his way under HQ and break into the Vault from beneath," Jason suggested, "like in that spy film where they stole the Crown Jewels."

"I doubt it," Dorian said. "The sensors in the Vault would alert us if someone drilled their way up into the Vault."

"If you three wouldn't mind, I need to write up my autopsy report," Mark said to them, and they left the morgue.

It was starting to go dark outside; Kate had taken Jason to the cafeteria upstairs. The cafeteria was on the main floor of the Underground at the end of a corridor facing the opposite side of the Hall of Records. Jason and Kate sat at the far side of the cafeteria. They had a chicken salad sandwich each and were eating when Jason decided to ask Kate something.

"Does your family know you work here?" he asked her.

Kate looked up at him. "No," she replied. "It's not easy for my family having a detective for a daughter, they're afraid half the time that one day they'll get a call saying I was killed in the line of duty, and if I told them the truth they'd be even more scared because I hunt down criminal vampires and other things that go bump in the night." She looked at Jason. "Sometimes, Jason, it's safer to tell a small lie than to tell someone you care about the truth."

Jason went quiet for a moment, then he spoke again.

"I just don't like lying to my family," he told her, "but I'm afraid of how they'd react if I told them I was a werewolf."

"They'll still love you, Jason," Kate said. "No matter what you are, your family will always love you."

They finished their dinner and went back out into the main hall. Kate checked her phone. "Well there's not a lot we can do now," she told him and put her phone away. "We might as well call it a day."

They made their way back up to the car park and were about to get in Kate's car to go home when the secretary came running out to them. "Doctor Barker needs to see you in the morgue," he told them both. "It's urgent!"

Kate and Jason got out of the car. Jason noticed the moon out in the night sky and how bright it was even in the dark.

"C'mon," Kate said to him and Jason stopped

staring at the moon and followed Kate back to the elevator. The secretary didn't go with them down to the morgue; he just went back to his desk the moment they stepped out of the elevator.

Mark was in the morgue. The body of the zombie had been taken away and he was cleaning the slab the zombie had been laid on. He was just getting round to cleaning his dissection tools when Kate and Jason walked in. Mark looked up at them.

"Is everything ok?" he asked them as they came over to him.

"You told the secretary that you wanted to see us," Kate said.

Mark looked at them both, confused. "No I didn't," he said. "I told you everything I found out when you were in here with Dorian earlier."

Kate was about to ask Mark something else when Jason began to groan. "Are you alright?" Mark asked Jason.

"No..." Jason managed to say, then collapsed behind the slab and Kate and Mark heard Jason's groans turn silent as his bones began to crack as they lengthened and his clothes tore – Jason was turning into a werewolf.

"Mark, get out now!" Kate told him, and they both began backing away towards the door. They reached the door and ran out of the morgue and locked the doors, then ran back down the corridor. Suddenly they heard the growling of the werewolf in the morgue. "Do you have you phone on you?" Kate asked Mark as they turned and ran down the next corridor.

"No, I left it in the morgue," he told Kate. They heard the doors to the morgue being torn off their hinges – the werewolf had got out.

They reached the stairs and began running up them. They could hear the wolf chasing after them, following their scent like the hunter it was.

* * *

"We've got to warn the others!" Mark said to Kate as they ran through the first door they came across. Thankfully this corridor was empty so no one would get hurt by the wolf. Kate got out her phone and handed it to Mark. "Try and get in touch with either Dwight or Dorian, they need to be warned!" she told him. Mark called the first number he saw and carried on running as it rang.

Dwight was in his office, writing reports up when his phone rang. It was Kate's number calling; he answered the phone. "What's wrong?" Dwight asked.

"Sir, it's me!" Mark replied. It sounded as though he was running.

"Mark, what are you doing with Kate's phone?" Dwight said, surprised.

"She gave it to me, sir. Jason's turned into a werewolf and he's running loose down here!" Mark explained. Dwight jumped to his feet.

"Where are you?" he asked Mark. "Me and Kate are heading for the cold case storage room!" Mark said. Dwight heard them run through a door.

"Lock yourselves in there, I'll warn everyone and get security to stun Jason before he gets anyone hurt or worse, killed." Dwight ended the call and picked up one of his office phones and flicked a switch on it. Dwight's voice was heard throughout HQ on speakers.

"Attention Underground, this is the Caretaker speaking. One of our people has turned into a werewolf and is running loose in the lower floors. If anyone is down there, lock yourselves in your offices and do not approach the werewolf under any circumstances. Security is heading down to tranquilise the wolf before it harms anyone. This is not a drill, stay in your offices and keep away from the corridors!"

Dorian came running into Dwight's office. "Is it true?" he asked Dwight.

"Yes," Dwight replied. "Jason has turned into a werewolf and is chasing Kate and Mark in the lower floors. I thought you and Kate gave him medication to stop him from turning into a wolf?"

"We did!" Dorian replied. "We stopped by his place so he could take his next set of tablets before coming back here this afternoon." Dwight loaded a tranquiliser gun with darts.

"Well they obviously didn't work. Someone must have tampered with them!"

Dwight handed a tranquiliser gun to Dorian. "Go down there with security and stop Jason before he gets anyone killed." Dorian took the gun and left Dwight's office. Dorian followed security down to the lower levels and separated from the group, then made his way to the cold case storage room.

* * *

Kate and Mark had locked themselves in storage. The room was big, not as big as the Hall of Records, but it was still big. Row after row of shelves filled with old case boxes which were either labelled solved or unsolved. Kate and Mark were kneeling behind a desk in the storage room; they could hear the wolf outside, sniffing at the door. Kate and Mark crawled their way down to one of the rows then got up and quietly began walking down the rows, looking for somewhere to hide. Suddenly there came a loud bang as the wolf tried to get into the storage room. Kate and Mark stopped, their hearts beating fast in fear and terror of the creature that was hunting them.

"There's a back door leading to a flight of stairs," Mark whispered to Kate. "It leads directly to evidence lockup."

"Then let's keep moving," Kate replied, and they continued creeping along the rows of shelves until they arrived at the back door. Suddenly they heard a crash as the doors were broken off their hinges and a growl echoed through the room. The werewolf was inside.

Chapter 26

The Break-In

Kate and Mark ran up the stairs and through the door leading into evidence lockup. They shut the door behind them and locked it, then they pushed a desk in front of it for good measure.

"That won't hold him," Mark said as they backed away from the door.

"No but it'll give us some time to get back upstairs," Kate told him, and they headed out of evidence lockup.

* * *

Dorian stopped outside the storage room. The doors had been torn down and he could hear the wolf inside.

Slowly he entered the storage room. His right hand had a tight grip on the tranquiliser gun. Dorian stepped into the storage room; it was dark, all the lights were off and it was empty and quiet.

Dorian slowly approached the first row and peered down it, nothing but darkness. Just above Dorian's head there came a low growl. Dorian gripped his gun then aimed upwards and he saw the wolf snarling at him. Suddenly there came an almighty bang from upstairs. This startled the werewolf and it dived off the shelf and bolted for the doors, ignoring Dorian. Dorian pulled out his phone and called Kate. It rang but no one answered. "C'mon, pick up!" Dorian muttered.

"Dorian?" Kate answered the phone. "What's going on up there?" she asked him.

"I don't know, I'm in cold case storage. Where are you?" Dorian said.

"We're on the next floor up," she told him. "We're in the zombie contagion ward."

"Stay where you are, I'm on my way," Dorian replied, and left.

Dorian was running up the stairs to the ZC (Zombie Contagion ward), when a security officer came tumbling down the stairs. He stopped halfway down and Dorian checked for a pulse – the officer was dead. He'd suffered a gunshot wound to the head. Someone had killed him and Dorian had an uneasy feeling he knew who was responsible. Dorian came to the top of the landing and a zombie came from round the corner, but Dorian shot him before the zombie had time to raise his gun.

Kate and Mark were up in zombie contagion ward. It was a big room, like a room from a police precinct. There were desks and computers, along with large boards with information pinned to them. A few members of the ZC unit were down here with them, they had locked and boarded the doors up so the werewolf couldn't get in. One of the people down there was on his computer, trying to get into the security cameras to see what was going on in the main hall.

"Someone's cut the power off on all the computers," Detective Alex Grissom said, and pushed away from his desk on his computer chair.

"Quiet! I think I hear someone coming!" a woman said, and there came footsteps down the corridor. Suddenly there was a tapping on the door.

"Kate, Mark, are you in there?" It was Dorian. Alex and a few other people helped Mark move stuff from the door, and after they unlocked it Dorian stepped in.

"What's going on up there?" Alex asked Dorian.

"Zombies," Dorian replied as he closed the door behind him. "Harfang's come for the Chalice."

"He can't have many zombies left after what happened at Heathrow," Kate said.

"More importantly, how the hell did they get past security?" Mark asked Dorian.

"I don't know, nothing like this has ever happened before," Dorian admitted. Alex looked at them then walked over to a gun rack.

"And you guys said that ZCU was useless these days," Alex said, and tossed Dorian a rifle.

"Is the werewolf still at large?" the woman asked Dorian.

"I'm afraid so."

"No worries," Alex assured everyone. "If Harfang is here then the wolf will pick up his scent and deal with him for us, then we tranquilise the werewolf and keep him detained until he turns back into a human."

"You're right," Dorian replied as Alex handed another rifle to someone, "but we're still going to have to close off the Hall of Records."

As soon as everyone had a rifle, Dorian devised a plan. "Harfang will be after the Chalice and to get it he'll have to go through the Hall of Records, but in an emergency like this, the Hall of Records is locked down so Harfang won't be able to get in, but that shouldn't stop him from getting what he wants."

Everyone looked at Dorian. "So our plan is this, we're going to sneak into the Vault and take the Chalice before Harfang can get his hands on it."

"Separate the lock from the key," Kate said.

"How are we going to get into the Vault?" a man in a blue tie asked.

"What Harfang doesn't know is that there's a secret entrance into the Hall of Records. I've only ever used it once and not many people know it even exists," Dorian explained. "It's two floors above us but we should be able to make our way to it unnoticed."

They were about to step out of the ZCU office when Alex turned to the rest of the ZCU. "There's probably the chance we'll run into some of our own people who have been bitten by zombies," he said, and silence filled the room... "If you see any Underground agents who have been bitten, don't hesitate to shoot them because they will definitely not hesitate to kill you." And with that, they stepped out of the office.

The second floor was directly below the main floor and the Hall of Records. The corridors were empty and quiet; they hadn't run into any zombies along the way, or the werewolf, but the corridor was littered with dead bodies – men and women who worked at the Underground. They had been shot through the head or the heart, some had even been torn apart, and it was difficult to tell whether they had been torn by a zombie or a werewolf. Dorian had told them that the secret entrance into the Hall of Records lay behind a portrait of Mary Shelly with Bram Stoker, Robert Louis Stevenson, and Washington Irving sat around a table at an old pub. They came to a corner and stopped at the end of the corridor. One of the walls had opened up, revealing a spiral staircase behind it, and on the wall was the painting Dorian had described.

"They can't have," Dorian muttered, and ran towards the open wall, the others close behind.

As they walked down the stairs, Kate noticed there were bullet holes in the wall, as though someone had been shooting at something.

"He can't have found it," Dorian said. Kate didn't know if he was talking to himself or to the others. "Only the founders knew about the secret passages. Van Helsing only ever told me."

"Was this passage ever on the original design plans?" Mark asked.

"Yes but it was a last-minute addition and those design plans of the Underground are locked away in the Hall of Records in Douglas and Oswald's office," Dorian explained.

"You don't think Harfang has someone on the inside, do you?" Kate asked.

"You mean in case we got the Chalice, he'd need

someone to help him get inside and steal it?" Dorian replied. "I wouldn't put it past him; he did something similar during World War Two."

They came to the top of the stairs; in front of them, the wall had been opened up again and led into the Hall of Records. The first thing they noticed was the trap door leading into the Vault was open; the hidden lock on the side of the bookcase had been found.

"Kate, with me! Mark, go check if the Librarians are alright," Dorian instructed, and Kate followed him down the trap door.

Mark and Grissom arrived at the Librarians' office. The door had been kicked in and Oswald was lying on the floor, motionless. "Is he breathing?" Grissom asked as Mark rushed over to Oswald's side. He checked for a pulse then looked up and gave a sigh of relief.

"He'll be fine but I need to get him to the medical bay."

"Don't mind me," Douglas said from behind his desk. He was on the floor, a bloodied handkerchief on his shoulder.

"Who did this to you?" Alex asked Douglas.

"Harfang," Douglas replied, "The undead git just walked in here and whacked Oswald on the back of the head with the butt of his gun, then he shot me in the shoulder and took my key and my key card. His apprentice took Oswald's."

"Apprentice?" Mark said, confused. "I didn't think Harfang had one."

"He was Harfang's spy, he must have sent him

here months ago to infiltrate us and find out where everything was and how to get into HQ," Douglas explained.

"Who?" Mark asked.

"That young secretary!" Douglas said.

Suddenly Mark remembered. "He was the one who sent Kate and Jason down into the morgue, he needed to make sure there was a distraction so Harfang could take us by surprise."

There came a low growl from outside the office.

"Crap," Mark said.

The werewolf was coming up to them.

* * *

Dorian and Kate walked down the stairs into the Vault, when they spotted a zombie. It was just stood there but the thing that was most worrying was the fact that it was wearing an Underground HQ security uniform. It turned around to face them. Its face was pale, with pale dead eyes and blood around its mouth. A bite mark could be seen on its arm. It groaned and lazily shuffled forwards towards them, a hungry look in its dead eyes, but before it could get any closer, Kate shot it in the head and the zombie dropped to the floor. Kate was quiet for a moment.

"Never thought I'd have to shoot one of our own," she finally said.

"You probably did him a favour," Dorian told her, and they walked into the reading area of the Vault. They passed the reading area and walked down into the Vault. They approached the electric fence, which was deactivated and the fence door was open. Dorian ran past the cabinets containing various artefacts and stopped when he saw the cabinet which housed the Chalice was wide open.

"Damn it!" Dorian said angrily, and turned to Kate. "Someone's helped Harfang get in here. I don't know who but someone has betrayed us."

"Dorian," Kate said. A thought had just occurred to her. "I think I know who betrayed us," she told him. Dorian looked at her. "When Jason and I were about to leave, the secretary came out and told us Mark needed to see us, but Mark said he never asked for us to come back. I didn't think about it until we came through the passage but now it all makes sense."

Dorian nodded. "The secretary would have had access to all information about the Underground," he said.

Kate spun around when she heard another groan behind her, past the electric fence. Zombies were slowly approaching.

"I count at least ten," Dorian said as he got out his loaded gun.

"How did we not see them when we came down here?" Kate asked Dorian.

"We were too busy focusing on getting to the Chalice, we probably didn't notice them amongst the cabinets," Dorian explained.

The zombies were getting closer; they were all Underground workers who had been bitten by Harfang's zombies, and without the zombie medication, or Medication Z, as it was referred to by some people, the zombies had become savage, flesh-eating monsters. Without thinking, Kate shut the fence door fast and the electricity was automatically switched back on. A zombie approached the fence and tried to break through but the moment the zombie placed its hands on the fence, it became shocked by one hundred and fifty volts of electricity running through the fence. Without a second to spare, Dorian shot the zombie through the head and it dropped to the floor, motionless. The smell of burnt flesh soon filled the air. The other zombies arrived at the fence and just stood there, looking at Dorian and Kate.

"Any ideas?" Dorian asked Kate.

"Not really," Kate replied. "I was just hoping they all shocked themselves on the fence really."

There were nine zombies remaining now, all of them making a horrible groaning sound like they were hungry, and Kate and Dorian knew what they wanted to eat.

* * *

The wolf slowly approached the door to the Librarians office. It sniffed the floor then turned to face everyone inside the room.

"I hope you have a plan," Douglas said to Grissom and Mark.

"Quite a good one actually," Mark said and pulled out a Taser. "I'm not allowed to use a gun anymore," he told Grissom and Douglas.

"Because of what happened in the park with Detective Joans?" Alex asked.

"I really don't want to talk about that now!" Mark

replied. Suddenly the wolf pounced at them but Mark was quick. He raised the Taser and fired it – wires shot out and stuck into the wolf and shocked him. The wolf landed on top of Mark, unconscious, with its tongue sticking out.

"That was your idea?" Douglas said, amazed at what had just happened.

"Oh bravo Doctor Barker, bravo," Alex said sarcastically.

"Shut up and help get this thing off me!" Mark gasped under the wolf's weight. Grissom smiled then helped move the wolf off Mark.

Two more people from the Zombie Unit came to help with the wolf and tied its arms and legs together. Mark had called for medics to come and take care of Oswald while he, Grissom, and Douglas went down to the Vault to see if Dorian and Kate were ok.

"Harfang knew about the secret passage," Mark informed Douglas as they walked down the trap door.

"Yes, he took me and Oswald by surprise. Not even me and him knew about that and we're the Librarians," Douglas remarked.

They carried on walking down the stairs until they arrived at the door. They saw a zombie on the floor with a bullet through its head. "Best way to kill a zombie is through the head," Grissom said, then stopped when he saw the uniform the zombie was wearing. He knelt down and looked at the ID badge.

"Did you know him?" Douglas asked as Alex took the badge off the body so he could get a better look.

"Yes, he'd been working here only a year, can't

believe he's gone." Grissom put the ID badge back on the body. "He had a wife and kids."

"Harfang knew we'd be forced to kill them," Mark told Alex, and they carried on walking.

They arrived in the Vault, only to see more zombies, crowded around the electric fence and on the other side of the fence were Kate and Dorian who were trying to keep the zombies away from the fence. One of the zombies turned and saw Mark and Alex, and began walking towards them. Four more zombies followed.

"I think I'll go back up and get help," Douglas said, and headed back to the stairs.

"Unbelievable!" Grissom said, and watched Douglas go.

"I know," Mark replied, then turned to Douglas. "Can I come with you?"

"Look out!" Alex shouted and Mark turned and saw a zombie coming towards him. Without hesitation, Mark shot the zombie in the head with his gun.

"Nice shot," Grissom remarked, then shot another zombie.

Slowly, Mark and Grissom worked their way towards Dorian and Kate, shooting down every zombie in sight before it even had a chance to get close to them. When they got close, Dorian called out to them, "You took your time in getting here!"

"Shut up," Grissom said as he and Mark took out another two zombies. It turned out there weren't only nine zombies in the Vault, there were fourteen, but by now they were down to at least seven or eight.

"There, one behind you!" Kate shouted to Mark and Mark spun around and fired.

Grissom shot another zombie in the head.

"I don't know about you but I'm running out of bullets," Mark told Alex after checking his gun.

"Same here," Alex replied.

The door to the Vault suddenly swung open and Dwight ran in carrying a shotgun; he was followed by four security guards.

"Get down there and finish the last of those zombies off," Dwight ordered, and security went to help Mark and Grissom.

"I do believe backup has arrived," Grissom said to Mark and carried on shooting zombies.

* * *

Crown was sat in his holding cell alone. He had heard Dwight on the speakers, telling everyone the boy had become a wolf, and he had heard the explosion when Harfang broke in. He smiled to himself, soon if not already, Harfang would have the Chalice and come to free him, this Crown was sure about.

The door to the room opened and footsteps could be heard. Crown got to his feet as Harfang approached his cell, a large case in his left hand.

"So you got the Chalice then," Crown said. Harfang smiled.

"Yes, my agent turned out to be useful after all. Now we begin the next stage in my plan…"

"Resurrect any and all deceased vampires and take over this country," Crown finished off.

"Indeed, old friend," Harfang said, and patted the case with his right hand. "You've been a loyal friend to me these past sixty-two years, Crown," Harfang told him.

"So are you going to let me out then, sir?" Crown asked Harfang, and Harfang looked up at Crown. The smile on his face vanished.

"I'm afraid not, Crown. Although I'm sure you didn't tell Dorian and the others anything about my plan, I trust you too much, but you getting captured has forced me to make many changes in my plans. Think of this as punishment, old friend." And with that, Harfang walked out of the room.

"You can't just leave me here!" Crown shouted from his cell. "After everything I did for you! Get back here and release me, Harfang!"

The door shut and the lights went out. Crown was alone in the dark.

Chapter 27

In the Med-Bay

All the zombies had been destroyed and dealt with, Dorian and Kate had been let out and were taken to the medical bay for treatment, along with Jason and anyone else who had been injured during the break-in. Jason had turned back into human form and was being treated in the med-bay, when he woke up he saw Kate and Dorian standing over him. Kate had chest pains after running down the countless corridors when Jason was a werewolf and had been given some water and painkillers. Dorian on the other hand, did not need medical attention.

"How are you feeling?" Kate asked Jason.

"Terrible," Jason replied weakly. "I can't remember what happened, one minute I was following you back to the morgue then I blacked out and woke up here." He looked up at them both. "I turned into it again, didn't I?" Jason asked them both.

"I'm afraid so," Dorian said.

"While you were down here in med-bay I called your mum. I said the reason you weren't back yet was because we had a system crash on all computers at

Scotland Yard and you and Kate had to go through all rough copies of the files that had been transferred onto computers," Dorian explained.

"Thank you," Jason said.

Dwight walked into the medical bay with the chief of security for the Underground. "I want security doubled at the entrances and I want you to have surveillance look over all security cameras to find out which way Harfang went when he left HQ," Dwight instructed the chief of security, then walked over to Jason's bed. "I've just spent the last hour giving instructions to security and overseeing any repairs needed to the Vault," Dwight said to Dorian. "We're going to have to change all the locks for the Vault of course, after this little affair."

Jason sat up. "Sir, I'm sorry if I caused any trouble while I was a wolf," he said to Dwight.

"It wasn't your fault, Wilson. Harfang needed a distraction to get into the base and he used you to get it," Dwight told him.

"Any idea how he got in?" Kate asked.

"The secretary let him in with his access card," Dwight explained. "We didn't know what was happening until Harfang's zombies stepped out of the elevators and threw that grenade. Eighteen of our security officers were killed before they even had a chance to react, and then the zombies went onto biting members of our staff."

"Before things got any more out of hand, the Hall of Records was sealed off and security and armed forces had been sent out to deal with the threat, but the infected members of staff became zombies themselves and were out of control. We had no choice but to shoot them."

"But Harfang found a way into the Hall of Records," Dorian said to Dwight.

"That's probably why he had his little spy plant himself in here," Dwight replied. "Someone on the inside who could mark out all the secret nooks and crannies this place has to offer."

The doors to the medical bay swung open and Mark walked through carrying a piece of paper. "I have good news and bad news," he told them all. "The good news is that I've found out how Jason's medication didn't prevent him from becoming a werewolf. The bad news is, Harfang knows where you live and he was more than likely at your house, Jason," Mark explained. "While you were unconscious I took some blood samples to see if you had any of the Anti-Wolf…"

"Anti-Wolf?" Jason interrupted. "That's what they call the medication I take? Anti-Wolf!"

"Sounded like a good name to give it when it was first made," Dorian said.

"But Anti-Wolf sounds stupid," Jason replied.

"Anyway," Mark carried on, "there was no Anti-Wolf in your system but there was salt. My guess is that Harfang got into your house and replaced your tablets with salt ones."

"How did he get into my house?" Jason asked, worried.

"We'll go down there now and ask your mum if anyone's been around today," Kate said to Jason.

"We?" Dorian asked.

"Yes, you and me," Kate replied as she headed for the door. Dorian watched her for a moment then followed on after her.

Chapter 28

What Do We Do Now?

Dorian's car pulled up outside Jason's house; the moon was still out and the stars were bright in the winter sky. Kate and Dorian got out of the car and walked up to the front door.

Kate knocked and Jason's mum answered the door. "Mrs Wilson," Dorian said.

"Is everything alright, detectives?" Mrs Wilson asked them both.

"Everything is fine, Mrs Wilson," Kate replied. "Jason had to stay behind and help finish off with the files," Kate lied.

"Actually that's one of the reasons we're here," Dorian told Mrs Wilson. "The reason all our computers crashed was because someone hacked into them." He took out a photograph from his coat pocket – it was a picture of Harfang. "Have you ever seen this man before, madam?" Dorian asked her, and showed Mrs Wilson the picture. She took it from him, her eyes widened.

"Oh my god. He was here this afternoon before Jason came back. He asked for directions and then asked to use the toilet," she explained to them.

"He's a dangerous person," Dorian replied. "He's wanted by the police for terrorism and multiple counts of murder."

"Oh my god!" Mrs Wilson said again, shocked. "I had no idea he was wanted by the police," she apologised.

"It's okay," Kate said, "he's good at fooling people, Mrs Wilson."

"Is it alright if we take a look around upstairs Mrs Wilson?" Dorian asked.

"Of course," Mrs Wilson replied, and let them in.

Dorian and Kate went upstairs; they went into Jason's room first and looked for his tablets. "Jason said he kept them in one of his desk drawers," Kate told Dorian as he searched the desk. He opened the top drawer. Nothing inside but a note book, pencil case, and a phone charger. In the second drawer there was a Nintendo 3DS, a normal DS, an old phone, and a green bottle with Jason's tablets in.

"Got them," Dorian said, and held up the tablets. He shut the drawer and handed them to Kate, who placed them in her pocket. Dorian looked around at Jason's room. On a shelf was a small TV, and on the shelves below were numerous games consoles. "They didn't have any of this stuff when I was his age," Dorian remarked as they left Jason's room.

"When you were his age Britain was still going through the Industrial Revolution," Kate told him.

"Thank you for reminding me how old I am," Dorian replied and smiled. They went into the guest room next, where Kate had been staying. As far as they could tell nothing had been taken. Jason's tablets were the only thing Harfang had taken. Kate shut the door to the guest room and followed Dorian downstairs. "Luckily nothing important was taken, Mrs Wilson," Dorian lied.

"Will you and Jason be returning here tonight, detective?" Mrs Wilson asked Kate.

"Yes, we're actually going back to pick him up now," Kate told her, then Dorian and Kate left the house.

When they arrived back at HQ, Dorian showed them the salt tablets and explained what Mrs Wilson had told them about Harfang's visit to Jason's house. "Well what do we do now?" Jason asked them all. "Harfang's got the Chalice, he was able to sneak into my house, and it looks as though he's won."

Mark was smiling, he shook his head and gave a small laugh.

"What's so damn funny Barker?" Dwight asked crossly.

"Harfang hasn't won yet," Mark told them, and he turned to Dorian. "We still have time."

"What does he mean?" Jason asked, and Dorian smiled back at Mark.

"Harfang wants the Chalice to resurrect all dead vampires," Dorian explained.

"Well technically they are already dead," Mark interrupted, but let Dorian carry on.

"He wants vampires to run this nation and possibly the whole world, but he won't be able to resurrect any vampires in London," Dorian said, and Kate figured out what he meant.

"He still has to go to Whitby," she said, "that's where all vampires are buried after they die, or are vanquished."

"So we're going to follow Harfang to Whitby, to stop him from raising an army of undead vampire-zombies?" Jason said, puzzled.

"Pretty much," Dorian replied, and walked out of the medical bay.

As soon as Jason's release forms were signed, Kate got him out of the med-bay and took him back to her car. Mark had got Jason a pair of scrubs to wear home due to the fact his clothes were torn; the doctors in med-bay had given Jason more Anti-Wolf tablets to take home, and he had taken one before leaving the med-bay.

"How are you feeling?" Kate asked him as they got into her car.

"I'm feeling better than I was," Jason admitted.

Kate pulled out of the parking space and made her way out of the car park. Jason hadn't spoken a word since they left HQ. "Are you alright Jason?" Kate asked him as they turned down a street.

"I'm fine," Jason lied to Kate.

"Jason, I'm a detective, I know when I'm being lied to," Kate replied.

Jason was staring out of the passenger side window of the car. "I just can't believe we lost," he told Kate. "We had the Chalice for a split second then it was taken and it's my fault, I should never have got involved in this."

"Jason it's not your fault any of this happened. Dorian and myself got you involved in this, not you. If it wasn't for you we wouldn't have figured out Harfang was after the Chalice until he'd taken it from the airport, but by getting to it before him we delayed his plans and now we're going to stop him, Jason, but we're going to need your help. Tomorrow morning we set off for Whitby to stop Harfang. Don't you see? This is no longer a murder investigation, it's something much bigger than that now. By tomorrow night our actions will decided whether or not this country belongs to the living or the dead," Kate explained and Jason looked at her. "Did you just quote *Abraham Lincoln: Vampire Hunter*?" he asked her.

"Yes. So? It's an awesome film," Kate replied, and they both laughed.

Chapter 29

To Whitby

With school closed for the rest of the week, Jason was able to go to Whitby with Kate and the others. Kate had explained to Mrs Wilson that they were going to Whitby to arrest Harfang and it would be good for Jason to be there to see and take part in the biggest arrest of the year. Mrs Wilson kissed Jason goodbye and told him to make it back to see his sister, Juliet, when she came back from college on Saturday to see them. Kate and Jason left the house and drove back to HQ where they had to meet the others, along with Dorian. Mark was going with them to Whitby, along with Dwight and some armed men in case they encountered any resurrected vampires.

Kate and Jason made their way to Dwight's office as soon as they arrived at the Underground. Dwight was waiting for them in his office along with Dorian.

"All the arrangements have been made," Dwight told Kate and Jason as they sat down next to Dorian. "We'll be taking the train to Whitby so as to reduce any suspicion in case Harfang has anymore agents watching HQ," he explained to the three of them.

"Do you really think Harfang has any more spies here?" Jason asked Dwight curiously.

"It's better to be on the safe side, Wilson," Dwight replied, and handed them all an envelope. "Your tickets are inside," Dwight said to them. "The Prime Minister wants Harfang caught as soon as possible and I'm sure I don't need to remind any of you what's at stake if we fail."

Kate, Jason, and Dorian left Dwight's office. "It seems Harfang didn't take everything last night," Dorian said to Kate and Jason as they walked down the corridor.

"What do you mean?" Kate asked him as they turned a corner.

"Crown's still in his cell," Dorian told them.

"What!" Kate exclaimed, and stopped outside the door to the forensic lab.

"Turns out Harfang isn't that loyal to his friends," Dorian commented.

"But doesn't he realise we may be able to get some valuable information from Crown?" Kate told Dorian.

"He hasn't told us anything yet but he may tell us now that Harfang's abandoned him," Dorian replied, and they headed off down to the holding cells.

Crown was the only prisoner they had in the cells; he sat on his bed, staring straight forward. He stood up when Dorian and Kate entered the room. They walked down three steps and approached Crown's cell. The door behind them opened again and Jason followed them into the room.

"So, Harfang left you behind," Dorian said to Crown, and he stepped closer to the bars so he could speak with Dorian.

"What the hell do you want, Gray?" Crown asked from behind the bars of the cell.

"We want to know what Harfang's planning," Kate told Crown, and Crown turned to her.

"Why should I help you?" Crown replied.

"Because if you don't help us we have plenty of war crimes we can charge you with," Dorian said, and Crown turned back to look at him.

"You'd love nothing more than to see me rot away in here, wouldn't you Gray?" Crown responded. "Even though you took everything away from me, my life and my family."

"You lost your family long before I killed you," Dorian told Crown. "They didn't agree with what you and the rest of the Nazis were doing," he explained. "Why do you think they never told you I was a spy? They were helping me get Jewish prisoners out of the prison camp under your control, and you were one of Harfang's servants."

Crown looked at Dorian then turned away and walked back to his bed. "I didn't exactly believe in what the Nazis believed in either, Gray," Crown said, and he sat down on his bed.

"Mr Crown," Jason said as he stepped forward, "we know what Harfang is planning and that he needs to go to Whitby to achieve it, but we don't know where exactly he'll be hiding and where he plans to perform the ritual. We need your help. You're the only one who knows what he's planning. If you help us then I promise you we'll let you make any plea bargain you want."

Crown looked at Jason for a minute, then he spoke. "I'll need a map of Whitby and a pen and some paper."

Kate nodded. "I'll have them sent to you at once," she replied, and went to find an officer.

"I'll have my plea bargain waiting for you when you get back," Crown told Jason, and lay back down on his bed. Jason and Dorian left the room.

"You know you're in no position to let our prisoners make bargains," Dorian said as he and Jason walked down the corridor.

"I guess you and Kate will have to handle his plea bargain then," Jason replied. The two laughed and headed back to Dwight's office.

They arrived at Kings Cross station at half ten and boarded the train to Whitby at quarter to eleven. Jason sat down with Kate as the train pulled out of the station, their bags at their feet.

"How long do you suppose we'll be there for?" Jason asked Kate as they passed numerous passengers on the platform.

"Two or three days at the most. I'm not sure," Kate replied.

As soon as they left the station, Dorian and Mark came to sit down with them. Dwight was busy talking on the phone with the armed forces unit and the Prime Minister. As soon as everyone was sat down, Kate took out the map of Whitby that Crown had marked out and laid it on the table in front of them. "Alright, this is where Crown said Harfang will most likely be hiding out." Kate pointed to an old monastery circled on the map.

"I know that place, it's not far from the cemetery," Jason told them. "I went there once on a school trip."

"Harfang will no doubt be expecting us," Dorian said as the train went through a tunnel, "so he'll probably begin the ritual tonight."

"That doesn't give us much time to make a plan," Mark said, and Kate looked at him.

"The plan is simple, we wait until night for Harfang to arrive then we arrest him before he resurrects any vampires."

"You make it sound so simple," Mark replied, "but I doubt that the plan will be that simple."

"It never is," Dorian said to Mark.

"By the way, do we know anything about the secretary?" Jason asked them.

"Well we know his name is Kevin Welker, died in 1934, came back to life as a vampire four days after his death. He had supposedly been stabbed to death with a silver knife in Nazi-occupied France during the Second World War," Mark informed them all, and showed them Kevin's file.

"He worked for us even back then!" Dwight said, alarmed, as he read the file. "How did we not have him on a list of workers from back then?" he asked them.

"He probably destroyed them after he returned back to HQ," Dorian replied. "It would explain how he knew so much about the Underground and why Harfang sent him in as a spy."

"But what I don't understand is why would one of your own fake his death and then betray the Underground by working with someone like Harfang?" Jason asked.

"Harfang might have manipulated Kevin into working for him, he's quite good at that," Dorian said to Jason, and the train went through another tunnel.

Chapter 30

The Ritual

It was quarter to two in the afternoon when they finally arrived in Whitby; the sea could be heard as the waves splashed against the rocks and sand on the shore, and the smell of salt water was in the air, just like you'd expect at the seaside.

The Underground had a house in Whitby they used for when agents had to come over to Whitby, and had spent the night. It was located on a street of houses in the town overlooking the docks where all the boats were. The front of the house looked old and in need of redecorating – the front door's dark green coat of paint was starting to peel off and on the front of the door was a small anchor. Dwight unlocked the door and everyone stepped inside. In front of them was a set of stairs leading to the next floor, and down the hall up ahead was a door leading into the kitchen, and the door on the left led to the living room. The walls were covered in flower wallpaper, something Jason didn't expect to see in the Underground's Whitby outpost, but it did make the house look unsuspecting at the least.

"Well, this is nice," Jason commented. He walked

down the hall and stopped just outside the door to the living room.

"Jason, what's wrong?" Kate asked, noticing something was off about Jason.

"Someone's been here before us," Jason told them. "I'm picking up a strong scent around here like I did at the church," he explained.

"The secretary must have told Harfang about this place," Mark said.

"Right, Dorian, go through the kitchen into the living room and see what Harfang's done in there," Dwight told Dorian, and Dorian went off into the kitchen. On the other side of the kitchen was a door that led in the living room. Dorian entered the living room and spotted what Harfang had done immediately – a thin line of wire stretched across the bottom half of the door that led into the hall. A small hook held the wire in place at one side, and on the other side, attached to the other end of the wire, was a bomb.

Dorian knelt down to examine the bomb. He looked for something that looked as though it deactivated the bomb, then he called out to the others in the hallway. "Whatever you do, don't come into the living room through the hallway door," he told them. "There's a wire hooked up to a bomb, opening the door will set it off and take out this house and the other houses on either side."

"Please tell me you know how to deactivate it," Kate called out from the hallway.

"I think so, but I'll need some help," Dorian replied.

"Hang on, I know a bit about bombs, I'm coming," Mark said, and headed down the hall, through the kitchen and into the living room. He knelt down beside Dorian to examine the bomb. "Is it linked up to a timer?" Mark asked Dorian.

"Not that I can see," Dorian said.

"Right, then our best bet is to try and defuse it," Mark instructed, and began running a finger down the side of the bomb, and stopped when he came to some wires.

"Do we have anything to cut these wires with?" Mark asked.

"There's a cupboard under the stairs, I'll go check there," Dorian replied, and got up and headed back into the kitchen.

Kate, Jason, and Dwight were waiting out in the hall when Dorian walked out of the kitchen and went into the cupboard.

"What are you looking for?" Jason asked. "I'm looking for something to cut the wires on the bomb with," Dorian explained as he searched through the cupboard. "Ha!" Dorian said, and picked up a pair of pliers, and Dorian returned through the kitchen.

Mark looked up at Dorian and took the pliers off of him. "Thanks."

Mark turned to the wires and looked at them carefully for a moment.

"Which wire do you think we cut?" Dorian asked him.

"I'm not quite sure," Mark replied and examined the wires carefully. If he chose the wrong wire, everyone except Dorian would be dead.

"I think we cut the blue one," Mark finally said.

"Are you sure?" Dorian replied.

"Positive, it's the blue wire."

"Alright then." Dorian turned to the door leading out into the hall. "It might be best if you three wait outside," Dorian called out.

"I hope you two know what you're doing," Kate said back, and they heard the front door open and the others step outside, then the door shut. They could hear Jason, Kate and Dwight walk away from the house, then Mark and Dorian focused on the bomb again. Carefully, Mark approached the blue wire with the pliers and brought them down on the wire then...

Kate, Dwight and Jason stood outside, waiting to see what would happen. Either Dorian or Mark would walk out the door and say it was okay to come in now, or the entire house and the two on either side of it would go up in flames. Jason spotted the door knob turn and the front door slowly opened. "We did it," Mark said as he stepped out of the house. Everyone gave a sigh of relief.

"Thank goodness," Dwight said, and they all went back inside the house. Dorian had removed the wire from the hallway door leading into the living room and the bomb had been taken away by two of the men from the armed force unit Dwight had brought as backup.

Everyone was now sat in the living room around the coffee table. "Well, we definitely know Harfang's here in Whitby," Kate said, and took a sip of her tea.

"It's a good thing Jason picked up Harfang's scent," Dwight replied.

Mark laid the map of Whitby out on the coffee table.

"I take it we're still heading to the cemetery tonight then?" Jason said as he looked at the map.

"Of course," Dorian responded as he walked out of the kitchen with his cup of tea. "Harfang will know by now we're here and have disarmed his bomb, so he'll want to begin the ritual as soon as the sun goes down."

"How does this ritual go anyway?" Mark asked, leaning forward in his chair.

"Well there are three steps to it, that's as much as I know, but one thing I do know is that not many people know how to perform the ritual," Dorian explained. "If I remember correctly, there are only three people in the entire world who know how to perform the ritual."

"One of them works for the Underground in America," Dwight added, "the second lives in Australia, and the third is dead."

"What!" Dorian gasped. "When did he die?" he asked Dwight.

"This morning. I got a call before we left, it was from the man's wife. She said he had died of a heart attack. I was aware, of course, the man had heart conditions but when he last contacted HQ, he said he was getting better."

"And you're only considering that odd now?" Jason asked, alarmed.

"We have more worrying things to deal with," Dwight replied. "In less than three hours the sun will start to set and Harfang will be getting ready to perform the ritual."

"How do we know Harfang didn't have the third person killed?" Mark asked, concerned with the strange death of the man.

"He's got a point, Richard," Dorian said. "Harfang could have tortured the man for information."

Dwight sat quietly for a full minute, then he spoke. "Alright, Barker. I want you, Joans, and Wilson to go over the coroner's report and any other pieces of information about the man. Dorian and I will start making plans for the cemetery tonight."

"Yes sir," Kate replied, and she, Jason, and Mark headed off.

On the second floor, there was a room that had been set up as a work station, fitted with computers. Jason and Kate were sat at two of the computers facing one another; they were reading up on the man who had died. His name was Henry Moore and he had lived in York with his wife and two children for eleven years. So far, nothing out of the ordinary.

"This is ridiculous," Kate said in frustration. "There has to be something odd or strange that led to his death."

"Hang on," Jason interrupted. Mark looked up from the file he was reading and looked at Jason. "It says here that three years ago, Moore had been fitted with a pacemaker for his heart condition, is it possible to make a person have a heart attack if you do something to the pacemaker?" he asked Mark.

"Actually I think it is possible." Mark stood up and walked over to Jason's computer. "When I first started working in the morgue, before I worked for HQ, one of my first cases was a woman whose pacemaker had caused her to have a heart attack. The police assumed it was the people who manufactured the pacemaker, but I discovered that her ex-husband had killed her, using his laptop to make her pacemaker give her a heart attack because she wouldn't sell her half of their company to him."

"Is it possible for someone to have done the same thing to Moore?" Kate asked Mark.

"Well if they had the serial code for Moore's pacemaker and if they knew what they were doing, then yeah, it's possible."

"Any luck?" Dwight walked into the room.

"We think someone made Moore's pacemaker give him a heart attack," Mark explained.

"Can someone cause a pacemaker to force a heart attack from a distance or do they need to be near the person to do so?" Dwight asked Mark.

"Well, it's not unheard of for someone to do something like this from a distance, but they could only be as far as in the next house for something like this to work, why?"

"After you three persuaded me to let you look into this case, I did some checking of my own. Look who lived on the same street as Moore in the next house," Dwight said, and handed them a piece of paper.

Kate took it and read it. "Kevin Welker," she read out.

"He likely moved there to try and learn the ritual from Moore, but Moore probably didn't like what Welker had in mind and refused to teach him the ritual, so Welker killed Moore and took everything he needed to know to perform the ritual," Dwight told them. "Mrs Moore called the police and said that three of her husband's books were taken from his study. They were most likely the books instructing a person to perform the ritual. I know for a fact not many of those books exist. Moore had three of them and the first person has one; he had it locked away in the Vault in the American HQ," he explained to the three of them.

At half four the sun began to set and everyone prepared for the events that would happen tonight. Kate and Jason were getting ready in their room. Kate had slipped on a dark maroon-coloured fleece jumper over her shirt and put on her Kevlar vest, Jason had put a fleece jumper on as well, and Dorian had been able to get hold of a Kevlar vest for Jason. He was putting it on while Kate checked her gun. "Have you still got that crossbow Dorian gave you?" she asked him as she put her spare gun in the holster on her right leg.

"Yeah, it's right here," Jason replied, and patted the box on the bedside table.

"You really don't have to be here, Jason. We dragged you into this. You can leave if you want and I promise no one will think any less of you," Kate told him.

"I want to stay and help you guys," Jason insisted. "Harfang used me as a distraction to slow you guys down twice now and I'd like to repay the favour.

Besides, Marry Creed had a family and I want to make sure Harfang's brought to justice for that."

Kate smiled and patted Jason on the shoulder. "Spoken like a true detective," she said.

* * *

It was quarter to six when they left the house; the plan was to make their way to the old ruins near the cemetery and stop Harfang before he could perform the ritual. Jason and Kate were to take a small group of men around the back of the monastery while Dorian and Mark took the main force to the front, and Dwight would have men set up on either side to prevent Harfang or any of his men escaping. Dorian and Mark were knelt down in the grass watching as Kate, Jason, and their men went round the back of the old building. "Do you think we'll apprehend Harfang tonight?" Mark asked Dorian.

"Probably not," he replied, "but we'll hopefully be able to stop his plans here though."

Kate and Jason crept along the side of the monastery; it had most likely been a beautiful building when it was first built but time had not been kind to it, and now the monastery was nothing but the ruined remains of a time long gone. They stopped at the edge of the building. Kate looked around the corner – zombies were patrolling the paths leading to and from the monastery and there wasn't any sign of Harfang or Welker anywhere.

"Anything?" Jason asked her.

"Only a few zombies on patrol," she informed him.

"I take it this is the part where we attack the zombies with our guns blazing," Jason said.

"Actually the plan is, we take out the zombies first so we have a clear shot at Harfang," replied Kate. She pulled out her walkie-talkie and called Dorian. "We're in position," she informed Dorian.

"On the count of three," Dorian responded through the radio. "One, two... three!"

Kate spun round the corner with her gun pointed at the zombies; Jason came round the corner with their men and stood beside Kate, his crossbow aimed at the nearest zombie. One of the zombies aimed his machine gun at Kate but before anyone could stop him, the zombie was shot down by Mark, who was running over to them with Dorian and their men. "Don't move... you're surrounded!" Dorian yelled at the zombies.

One by one, the Zombies dropped their weapons to the ground and raised their hands in the air. "Where's Harfang?" Kate asked them, but the zombies remained quiet.

"Check the monastery," Dorian told her. Kate gestured to Jason and the two of them went to check out the old monastery. A few minutes later Jason called for Dorian and Mark.

"Guys, you're going to want to see this."

Dorian and Mark left the men to finish gagging and tying up the zombies so they could do no more harm. When they reached the monastery, they found what was left of a room; a coffin lay in one corner and crates were scattered throughout the rest of the room. The lid to one of the crates had been opened and inside were bottles of blood. What they noticed immediately was that three bottles were missing. "Do any of the three stages of the ritual require blood?" Jason asked, as he picked up one of the bottles to examine it.

"Yes. If I remember correctly, the first stage requires it." Dorian took the bottle off of Jason to look at it. "He must already be preparing to perform the ritual." Dorian put down the bottle of blood and picked his gun back up off the crate. "C'mon!" They left the abbey.

Suddenly they heard thunder up in the sky; a storm was brewing, and over the wind they could hear shouting. "I think that's Harfang!" Mark shouted over the noise of the storm. Dorian signalled to the soldiers to follow him. They needed to move fast now – Harfang had started the ritual.

Chapter 31

Blood of the Chalice

The team was heading back to the church as fast as they could. Harfang's voice got louder as they got closer. "We'll never make it in time!" Kate told Dorian.

"We have to move faster!" Dorian replied.

Harfang was speaking in Latin. Jason didn't understand what was being said but he knew it had to be something bad. Dorian got out his phone as they ran and called Dwight.

"Dwight, he's starting the ritual!" Dorian informed Dwight.

"I know," Dwight replied. "I'm heading to the church with my men now."

Dorian hung up and carried on running towards the church.

Jason tried as best he could to keep up with the team; his chest was hurting and his legs were aching. "We're almost there now," Kate told him. She held onto his hand and they kept going. The church wasn't far away now.

Harfang could be seen outside the church; his hands were held up in the air. In his right hand was a vial, and the Chalice stood on a stone slab. Harfang began pouring the blood from the vial into the Chalice and as the blood touched the Chalice, it began to boil, and steam began to rise from the Chalice...

Suddenly Jason heard something – the metallic click from a machine gun. "Get down!" Jason cried, and then, they heard the sound of a machine gun being fired.

Everyone got down and was able to find cover before anyone was hit. "Who's firing?" Mark called over to Dorian from behind a rock.

"It's Welker," Dorian said. He raised his head slightly so he could see Welker from behind the stone fence to the church. "It's over Welker!" Dorian shouted. "Surrender now or we'll have no choice but to shoot you."

Welker ignored Dorian and continued firing at them. With no other alternative, Dorian stood up and fired back at Welker. Dorian got hit in the shoulder but before Welker could shoot him a second time, Dorian shot him in the chest and Welker scuttled off into the shadows.

"Thanks for the warning," Mark said to Jason as they got up off the ground.

"One of the advantages I suppose, of being a werewolf," Jason said, "we get sharper hearing."

"Are you alright?" Kate asked Dorian as she helped him up.

"I'll be fine," Dorian assured her, "just get to the

church and stop Harfang, hurry!"

Mark led the rest of the way to the church; they were nearly at the church when they heard the first of the graves burst open.

Earth and dirt was flung everywhere as a decayed hand rose out from the grave and pulled the rest of its decaying body out of the ground.

The corpse was a horrific sight to be seen, decayed and scarred beyond recognition of who this poor soul might have once been before. "Kill them!" Harfang cried from the front of the church. "Kill them, my brethren. Kill them and do my bidding. Leave no survivors!"

"Is he as dramatic and mad as they get?" Jason asked Kate.

"Sadly, no," Kate replied.

The decayed vampire slowly made its way towards them, scraping its left leg along on the church path. "Screw this," one of the soldiers said, and shot the vampire through the head twice, but it didn't kill the creature.

"I don't get it," said Jason as they backed away. "I thought silver is meant to kill vampires?"

"It does," Mark responded as he tried to shoot the vampire dead but nothing happened, except that more vampires were rising out from their graves.

"Then something's not right," Jason said. He looked over to where Harfang stood. "The Chalice!" he cried. "The Chalice must be keeping it alive!"

"Right, Jason, with me, you lot stay with Mark and try and hold off as many as those things as you can,"

Kate instructed, and then she and Jason headed off around the side of the church.

* * *

Mark and the soldiers took cover behind the stone fence of the church, desperately trying to take out the vampires. "We need to give Kate and Jason enough time as possible, keep firing," Mark told the soldiers, but no matter how many times they fired at the vampires, they kept coming. Then, one of them pounced on Mark, pinning him to the ground. Mark tried to fight back but the vampire was too strong and it moved in for the kill, about to rip out Mark's throat, when there came the sound of a shotgun and the vampire's head exploded, splattering blood, bone, and brain matter all over Mark. Mark looked up to see who had fired.

"One of these days I won't be around to look out for you, Barker," Dwight said, a smoking shotgun in his hands. Mark pushed the vampire's body to one side and got up off the ground and tried to wipe as much of the vampire's head off of him.

"Oh god," Mark said, and knelt down to be sick.

"You're a doctor for goodness' sake," Dwight said. "You're supposed to be used to this kind of stuff."

"I'm not used to people's heads exploding in front of me," Mark replied, and vomited again.

"Err, sir?" one of the men said to Dwight. "Is it me or is that body still moving?"

Dwight looked over to the headless corpse and to his horror, the body was getting back up on its feet. "Oh bloody hell," Dwight said, and Mark glanced over at the vampire.

"Oh my god!" he gasped and stepped back and picked his gun up off the ground. "Try shooting its legs!" Mark told Dwight, and Dwight fired upon the vampire a second time.

* * *

Kate and Jason slowly made their way around the side of the church, making their way closer to Harfang and the Chalice. "If I'm right, then that blood in the Chalice is stopping these creatures from dying," Jason explained, and turned to look at Kate.

"What's the plan then?" Jason asked her.

"I'll distract Harfang and you get over to that Chalice as fast as you can and empty it of all the blood before any more vampires are resurrected from the grave."

They carried on up the side of the church. When they reached the edge, Kate went around the corner with her gun in hand but Harfang wasn't there. The Chalice was just sitting there unguarded and then… *wham!* Harfang had snuck up behind Kate, grabbed her by the throat, and pinned her to the wall. "Did you seriously think I would not have suspected something as foolish as this, detective?" Harfang asked Kate as he tightened his grip around her throat.

"Let her go!" Jason demanded, pointing his crossbow at Harfang, and all Harfang did was laugh.

"Or what, you'll shoot me, boy? You couldn't hit me if you were any closer," Harfang mocked.

"Suit yourself," Jason said, and fired the crossbow. The silver arrow sped through the air and slashed

Harfang across his left cheek. Harfang howled in pain and let go of Kate.

"You insolent little thing!" Harfang said to Jason, his hand covering his cheek as blood ran down it. Kate got up and ran for the Chalice, but Harfang grabbed hold of her and sunk his teeth into Kate's leg.

"Arrr!" Kate cried out in pain. Jason ran over to them and kicked Harfang in the face, forcing him to let go of Kate.

"I will make you regret this Mr Wilson!" Harfang barked at Jason in anger.

Kate picked up her gun and got back up. Leaning against a gravestone, she pointed her gun at Harfang. "Jason, the Chalice quick!" she told him, and Jason made a run for the Chalice.

"No!" Harfang cried and tried to stop Jason, but Kate shot Harfang in the shoulder.

Harfang collapsed to the floor, blood oozing out of his wound. Jason ran to the slab where the Chalice stood, but someone dived on Jason and pinned him to the ground. Jason looked up and saw Welker on top of him, both of his hands around Jason's throat.

Jason tried gasping for breath but Welker's grip was too tight. Jason searched around on the ground with his free hand and rested it upon one of the silver arrows for his crossbow. Jason grabbed hold of the arrow and stabbed it into the side of Welker's head, killing him instantly. Jason pushed Welker's dead body off of him and got up off the ground; he dived for the Chalice and pushed it off the slab. The hot blood spilled out of the Chalice and sizzled on the stone path. Steam rose from the sizzling blood and then all the noises of corpses breaking free from their graves stopped, and instead, the sound of a vampire dropping to the ground as it was shot through the head could be heard.

Chapter 32

A Fight with a Vampire

"They've done it!" Mark cried as another vampire dropped dead on the grass. "They've broken the power the Chalice had over these corpses."

"We've still got this lot to deal with though," Dwight said as they carried on shooting the vampires that were still trying to kill them. "Where the bloody hell is Dorian?" Dwight asked Mark.

"He got shot in the shoulder so he stayed behind near that stone back there; Dorian said he would join us once his shoulder's healed," Mark explained. Dwight turned back.

"Well he's not there now," he told Mark. Mark turned back and saw that Dorian was gone.

* * *

Harfang threw himself at Jason and placed both hands around Jason's throat. "You've ruined everything!" Harfang yelled at Jason. His fangs could be seen now as Harfang spoke. "Of all the things to ruin everything I had planned, it was a werewolf. Not even in wolf form, just some pathetic kid who got involved in the wrong crowds. I am going to make you suffer for this, child!"

Harfang leaned in closer to Jason.

"Do you know, vampire bites are lethal to a werewolf? A vampire's bite is like poison to werewolves. It won't kill you at first, but within a day you will start to feel pain and agony which will last several days until you come to a very sudden and most painful death." Harfang opened his mouth, his fangs were sharp and jagged. He began to move in for the kill when, *BANG!* Harfang whipped his head around to see who it was.

Dorian was standing behind them, a gun in his hand. He had just fired into the air to get Harfang's attention.

"You just couldn't let someone else catch me, could you Gray?"

Harfang let go of Jason and turned to face Dorian.

"It ends this time, Harfang," Dorian told Harfang. "You're not getting away again that easily."

Suddenly, without warning, Harfang hit Dorian in the chest, making Dorian lose his balance and fall to the ground.

Harfang made a move for the Chalice but Jason snatched it up before Harfang could grab it. "Not so fast, Harfang," Kate said, her gun pointed at Harfang.

"No doubt, you've got silver bullets in that gun, detective," Harfang said to Kate.

Kate fired but all that came out of the gun was a clicking sound.

"Or at least you would if you had your ammo,"

Harfang went on. Then, Harfang threw a stone at Kate that narrowly missed her head. Dorian dived at Harfang but Harfang was too fast for him; he avoided Dorian and grabbed hold of him from the back of his jacket and flung Dorian straight through the stained glass window of the church, and Dorian went crashing into a row of seats.

Jason tried to make his way to the church door to help Dorian out but Harfang blocked his path. "Give me the Chalice, boy," Harfang said calmly. Jason backed up against the stone slab. "I shall only ask you one more time. Give me the Chalice." Harfang was beginning to get impatient with Jason. Jason quickly grabbed the empty glass vial from the slab and smashed it on the stone then, before Harfang had time to react, Jason slashed the broken vial across Harfang's face. "Arrr!" Harfang screamed. Jason made a break for the church but Harfang grabbed hold of Jason by the shoulder and threw him across the courtyard. The Chalice was still tightly gripped in Jason's hand.

Jason hit a mound of dirt just below a tree. He looked up at the plant and remembered the old vampire films he usually watched with his mum on Halloween. Vampires could be killed with wooden stakes, of course! He realised that to kill Harfang, he would need a stake from the same tree used to make the wood for the cross Jesus was crucified on, but it might be enough to slow Harfang down. Jason grabbed the lowest branch he could find and snapped it off the tree. He turned and saw Harfang lunging towards him.

Jason raised the wooden stake and drove it into

Harfang's chest.

* * *

Although no more vampires were rising from the grave now, Dwight and his men were still surprisingly outnumbered, but now that the vampires could be killed, the soldiers were evening the odds easily. "Don't let them get too near to you!" Mark told the soldiers as they continued firing at the vampires. The night air was filled with the sound of gunfire and nothing else could be heard over it. Dwight knew that the police would be showing up to investigate the gunfire soon and he hoped his agents back in the town would be able to delay them long enough for Dwight and his team to clean up matters at the church.

"Look out, sir!" shouted one of the Underground officers. A vampire was diving at Dwight but the officer pushed him out of the way in time and the vampire attacked the officer instead. Dwight turned and shot the vampire in the head, killing it instantly.

"Are you alright, officer?" Dwight asked as he helped the officer up on his feet.

"No sir," the man replied. His right hand was over his left arm and blood was oozing out of his bicep. "That bastard vampire bit me in the arm."

"You, medic!" Dwight shouted across the yard. One of Mark's field medics came running over to them. "Take this man and get him looked at and patched up right away," Dwight ordered the medic.

"Yes sir," she replied, and helped the officer out of the church cemetery and over to a small medical station Mark and his medics had set up not long ago.

Dwight rushed over to help a few more of his team and then carried on fighting off the vampires.

* * *

Kate searched for her bullets but couldn't find them; Harfang had no doubt removed the bullets without her knowing when he pinned her to the wall. "Kate!" Dorian shouted from inside the church. "Catch!" Dorian tossed out his gun through the broken window. Kate grabbed the gun and rushed off to help Jason. She had seen him stab Harfang with a branch.

Harfang howled in pain; blood ran down his suit. Slowly and painfully, he pulled the branch out of his chest. His eyes were a blood red, filled with anger. He snarled at Jason and raised the branch, ready to stab Jason in retaliation when Kate shot him in the shoulder, BANG! She shot him again in the same shoulder; this gave Jason a chance to get away.

Harfang tried to grab him but Kate shot Harfang in the left leg below the kneecap. Harfang slowly turned to face Kate. His face was twisted in pain and anger – the silver bullets felt as though they were on fire inside Harfang's shoulder and left leg. He showed his fangs again, snarled, and began to approach Kate. Kate tried firing her gun again but the gun jammed, She backed away, but Harfang was getting closer.

Inside the church, Dorian noticed a stained glass window of Jesus on the cross; it had obviously been added to the church recently. Dorian had an idea. He looked around for a light switch and spotted one at the back of the church. He ran to the end of the church and quickly began flicking every switch he saw, and with a great flash of light, the inside of the church lit up and the light hit the stained glass window, reflecting the colour and the light outside.

Harfang got closer to Kate as she tried to unjam her gun when suddenly, the church lit up inside and the light reflection from one of the stained glass windows shone brightly in the image of the cross. "Arrr!" Harfang cried out in pain as the light from the church hit him. The light from the cross reflected on his face and his skin began to blister.

Kate finally unjammed the gun and fired upon Harfang one more time, hitting him in the right leg this time, forcing him to fall to the ground and hit his head on a grave stone, knocking him unconscious.

"Is he dead?" Jason asked Kate, his crossbow pointed at Harfang's head.

"No, just knocked out," Kate told him.

Dorian climbed out of the church through the broken window. He spotted Harfang on the ground and rushed over to Kate and Jason. A smile broke out on his face. "Good job you two," Dorian said.

"Kate did most of the work," Jason told Dorian. "I only slowed him down a little."

"You're being too modest, Jason," Kate replied, smiling.

"There's still one, small piece of business we have to take care of," Dorian told them both, and got out a pair of silver handcuffs and tossed them to Kate; Kate knelt down and began handcuffing Harfang.

Chapter 33

Finishing Things Off

The path leading up to the church was stained with blood; as more and more of the vampires were killed, the less there were to deal with. It had been a long and difficult night but it wasn't over yet – several of the Underground soldiers had been killed by the vampires, either ripped to shreds or had their throats ripped out.

Dorian and Kate carried Harfang back to the others while Jason carried the box which he had put the Chalice back in, and he felt sore all over his body. Kate was limping, due to the bite marks in her right leg. The only one not in any form of pain was Dorian; his shoulder had healed up and apart from the bullet hole in his coat, Dorian looked as though nothing had happened to him. When they arrived at the bottom of the cemetery, Dwight and his men had nearly finished off all the vampires. As two more vampires were slain, Kate and Dorian dragged Harfang's body down the path towards the team. Mark spotted them and headed over to them.

"You got Harfang!" was the first thing Mark said.

"It wasn't easy," Kate responded, as she and Dorian let go of Harfang so two Underground officers could drag him back to the van.

"If you'll come with me, I'll get someone to look at your injuries," Mark told Jason and Kate, and without any response they both followed him back to the medic stand. Dorian went off with the two officers, to make sure when Harfang came round, he wouldn't try to escape.

As the last of the vampires was slain, Dwight ordered his team to gather up the bodies and burn them. He also wanted an armed escort to accompany Harfang back to Underground along with what was left of his zombie servants. Dwight wasn't taking any chances with Harfang. Dorian even volunteered to join the armed escorts just to be sure Harfang didn't make any attempt at escape.

"Where will you hold him?" Jason asked Dwight as the other wounded members of the team were seen to.

"Well he'll remain in the Underground until his trial and then will be taken to one of our special prisons that we have for people like Harfang," Dwight explained.

Kate came limping over to them. Her leg had been bandaged up and she seemed to look a lot better than before. "Good job catching Harfang you two," Dwight complimented both of them.

"Thank you sir," Kate responded, smiling. She checked her watch – it was already nearly three o' clock in the morning, "If it's alright with you, sir, I'd like to go back to the house and get some sleep," Kate told Dwight.

"Me too," Jason added.

"Alright," Dwight said, "but I want your report handed in as soon as we get back to London, Joans."

"Yes sir," Kate replied, and with that, Jason and Kate headed back into town.

Chapter 34

Back Home

The next day, they caught the train back home and arrived back in London at half eleven. Now that Harfang was in custody, Kate didn't have to stay with Jason's family anymore and could move back into her apartment.

Once she had packed up, Kate said goodbye to Mrs Wilson and thanked her for her hospitality.

"Jason told me you caught the man who had been to the house the other day," Mrs Wilson said to Kate.

"Yes," Kate replied happily. "He was planning to sell crucial information to a terrorist group," she lied.

"Thank goodness you got him then," Mrs Wilson said, and Kate stepped out of the front door.

Jason was sat out on the bench in the front garden, reading Washington Irving's *The Legend of Sleepy Hollow.* "I assume this story is also based on real events?" Jason asked Kate as he looked up at her from his book.

"I haven't the faintest idea," she confessed to him, "all I know is it's inspired by a German huntsman and a Hessian soldier." Kate put her bag in the boot of her car then turned back to Jason. "I take it you're not interested in joining the Underground," she said. Jason closed his book and looked at her.

"I, I just don't know what I want to do," Jason admitted. "I don't like lying to my family about what I'm doing and about who I am now."

Kate smiled. "I understand," she told him and got in her car. Kate lowered the passenger side window. "Just remember, the job is still open if you want it," and Kate drove off.

Jason's sister, Juliet, arrived home later that day; she asked how Jason was feeling and looked at his bite marks. After dinner, they all watched television and listened to how Juliet was doing at college. After that, they decided to call it a night and go to bed. The next day, Jason was sat at his bedroom desk, reading the news on his laptop. It was about political stuff mostly, and a celebrity who had gone into rehab. He found that he was bored about hearing what felt like the same things every single day in the news, and only then did Jason realise how much he missed the world he had spent the last week in, and wanted to go back to it.

He had Kate's number in his phone; he could call and tell her he'd like to join the Underground. His mother and sister already thought he was doing a work experience course at Scotland Yard, and if he decided to join the Underground, he could say that Scotland Yard wanted him to stay on the work experience course longer.

Kate arrived at his house in the afternoon to pick

Jason up. He kissed his mum and his sister goodbye, then went out and got into Kate's car. "So you decided to stay then?" Kate asked as Jason put his seatbelt on.

"Yes, I decided to stick with you lot for a little while longer," Jason replied. "Besides, after everything I've been through, everything I now know, it's impossible to just walk away from it and I want to know more about this new world I'm a part of, and what else is out there," he admitted.

Kate looked at him and smiled. "It's good to have you as part of the team, Jason," and Kate drove off back to the Underground.

When they got there, everything was back to normal. It looked as though no one had ever broken into the Underground or a werewolf had been running loose. Oswald and Douglas were talking as they walked down the stairs from their office and into the Hall of Records; people were passing through the hallway with files, notes, and books. Two cleaners were polishing the statue of Professor Van Helsing.

"Joans, Wilson!" an Underground agent shouted to them from across the hall. "The Caretaker wants to speak with you."

Kate and Jason headed down the corridor that led to Dwight's offices – a few security officers nodded to them and a couple of Underground agents said, "Good job," to them for arresting Harfang. They arrived at Dwight's office and Kate knocked on the door.

"You wanted to see us, sir?" Kate asked.

"Yes Joans," Dwight said. "Come in, both of you."

Kate and Jason stepped inside and closed the door behind them.

Chapter 35

Partners

"Take a seat," Dwight said to them both. Jason and Kate sat down on the chairs in front of Dwight's desk. "Harfang's trial date has been set for this Thursday approaching," Dwight informed the two of them. "Naturally, as the lead detective on the case, you'll have to go up on the stand, Joans."

"I know, sir," Kate replied.

"Also, the Prime Minister is pleased with how you handled the case, detective, and he believes that Mr Wilson should stay on at the Underground," Dwight said. Kate opened her mouth to speak. "And I for one agree with him, detective," Dwight interrupted. "So much so, that I think, he should be your new partner."

"But sir, I thought you said I need to be evaluated before I can officially work for the Underground?" Jason replied.

"We'll deal with that later, but first, Marry Creed's parents are here to collect her body. I want you both to meet them and show them down to the morgue."

"Yes sir." Kate nodded and the two stood up and walked out of Dwight's office.

Kate and Jason walked down the corridor, back to the main hall. Neither Kate nor Jason said anything until they were outside the Hall of Records. Kate looked at Jason. "So," she said to Jason, smiling, "it would seem we're partners now."

"It sounds that way," Jason replied, smiling back.

"I just heard you've been hired here." Dorian came walking up to the two of them. "Congratulations," he said, and shook Jason's hand.

"I take it you know, Jason's been assigned to be my new partner?" Kate asked Dorian.

"It was me who suggested it to Dwight," Dorian admitted. "I think you two work really well together and I enjoyed working with the both of you. My only regret is that I won't be able to work with you both for a while."

"Why?" Jason asked, confused.

"I'm leaving the British Underground for a while," Dorian told them both. "Harfang's arrest got me thinking. I've been hunting him my whole life. I used to think I wouldn't know what to do after I arrested Harfang but now, I think I do." Dorian loosened his grip on his walking stick. "I'm going to Australia for a year or two," he told them. "Of course, when I say a year or two, it usually means twenty to fifty years but not this time. Besides, the Australians have an Underground of their own. I might go and visit them and offer a helping hand."

Kate held out her hand. "It was an honour to work with you, Mr Gray," she said, and Dorian shook her hand.

"The honour was all mine, Detective Joans." He turned to Jason. "And it was a pleasure to meet you too, Jason Wilson," Dorian added, and after shaking Jason's hand a second time, Dorian walked over to the elevators and left.

"Once again, I am so sorry for your loss, Mr and Mrs Creed," Kate said to Marry Creed's parents as they left the morgue. Mr Creed, eyes full of tears, nodded, and his wife held onto his arm as they walked out of the morgue.

"I'll never get used to that," Jason confessed as soon as they were gone.

"I still haven't," Kate told him.

"How's your leg by the way?" Mark asked Kate as he finished signing some paperwork.

"It's feeling a lot better now, thanks to you," she said.

Suddenly, the morgue phone rang.

"Hello," Mark said as he answered the phone. "Yes they're here, sir. I'll tell them at once. Of course, sir." Mark put the phone down. "That was Dwight," he told Kate and Jason. "He's just received word that a creature has been sighted in the pond at Hillsborough Park in Sheffield. Apparently, it's stalking girls who attend Hillsborough College."

"We're on it," Kate said, and Jason followed her out of the morgue.

"Looks like your evaluation will have to wait," Kate told Jason as they walked up the stairs back to the main hall.

"Do you think this creature may be dangerous?"

Jason asked as they entered the main hall and approached an elevator.

"There's always the chance," Kate said.

"Then it's a good thing I brought my crossbow…"

"Wilson!" Dwight shouted from across the hall. "I think you left this in my office," and held up the case containing Jason's crossbow.

"Yeah, you're probably going to need that." Kate laughed.

Look out, for the next instalment in the Underground case files:

The Book of Monsters

14845747R00119

Printed in Great Britain
by Amazon.co.uk, Ltd.,
Marston Gate.